# DEEP OCEAN SIX

## DEFENDERS OF THE OVERWORLD

## BOOK 4

Nancy Osa

*Two if by sea . . .*

Sky Pony Press
New York

First Edition

This is a work of fiction. Names, characters, places, and incidents are from the author's imagination and are used fictitiously.

Sky Pony Press books may be purchased in bulk at special discounts for sales promotion, corporate gifts, fund-raising, or educational purposes. Special editions can also be created to specifications. For details, contact the Special Sales Department, Sky Pony Press, 307 West 36th Street, 11th Floor, New York, NY 10018 or info@skyhorsepublishing.com.

Visit our website at www.skyponypress.com.

10 9 8 7 6 5 4 3 2 1

Library of Congress Control Number: 2015953059

Cover illustration by Stephanie Hazel Evans
Cover design by Brian Peterson

Print ISBN: 978-1-5107-0323-0
Ebook ISBN: 978-1-63450-0324-7

Printed in Canada

# DEEP OCEAN SIX

For Marc and his fellow English teachers

. . . with apologies to Sara and her colleagues, for the "librarian" joke.

# CHAPTER 1

**A**S THE SUN DOVE INTO A HORIZON WASHED IN gold and pink, Battalion Zero's quartermaster sat discussing the evening's agenda with the sergeant at arms in the camp stable yard. Their four cavalry mates worked nearby. The pale, thin teenager faced the tattooed mercenary and said earnestly, "Unless I am wrong—and I'm never wrong—this minecart thing holds the key to our success." Jools ran a hand through his short, wavy brown hair and waited for Turner to praise his foresight.

Turner scratched his tanned belly through the rip in his T-shirt. "Yeah, well. Nobody's perfect."

Jools grimaced. If his calculations were correct, before the moon rose, the cavalry group would have simultaneously demolished a mob of silverfish, slain the griefer controlling them, and disarmed a bomb that threatened the lives of more than a hundred unsuspecting villagers. That was pretty close to perfect. The detail-minded quartermaster could scarcely remember the last time one of his plans hadn't worked. In fact, he could probably count his failures on one hand.

"Being not-right is not the same as being wrong," Jools pointed out. "Let's see. When have I ever been not-right? Well, there was the time I decided I could fly if I made wings out of plastic cling film . . . that was a flop, to say the least. Although, if I'd kept at it, I daresay the next aerospace breakthrough would've been mine. . . . Then, there was the blasted science-class volcano that didn't erupt, but only because I deemed the probability of such an explosion less than one hundred percent. Seems I was the only one in my class who wanted it to be realistic." He hiked up the sleeves of his tweed jacket, which he'd paired with loose jeans, and thought some more. "Ah, yes. My plan to circumnavigate the Overworld by walking in a straight line did have one obvious flaw. But I couldn't have foreseen that when I entered the game as a newbie."

"What? That the Overworld ain't round?"

"Touché. Other than those forgettable events, my record is flawless. So this scheme should be, as well."

"Flawless, huh?" Turner gave him a skeptical look. "Sayin' you're always lucky in love? I don't recall seein' a significant other on your arm the whole time I've known you." He paused. "And horses don't count."

The muscled mercenary sat back on his dirt block with a smug expression on his face.

*Ouch. That smarts.* Jools had been thinking about his pet, but only because it was time to give Beckett a hoof trim. "It's not too late for me to let *your* old lady know about your new girlfriend," Jools shot back. He'd been saving the threat for just such an occasion.

This didn't faze Turner. "Rose? Yesterday's news, Quartermaster. That girl ain't nowhere near a friend. Never was. Sundra don't need to know about her. Why not talk about your conquests instead? An' I don't mean zombies and skeletons."

Jools wasn't used to Turner's barbs actually snagging on his emotions. *How could he know my rubbish classmates once voted me "Most Likely to Remain a Bachelor"? I may be a tad lonesome, but it's tough to meet girls in a world where they randomly generate. Not like I can nip off to the armor-dying salon, or wherever it is females congregate.*

Still, Turner seemed to do all right. Wounded, Jools turned the conversation back to the problem at hand. "My real *conquests,* as you put it, consist of air-tight strategies that result in a payoff of some kind. This particular one will gain us the priceless virtue of world peace. Care to argue with that?"

Turner scowled. "Look, pal. Peace is overrated. I think we both know, deep down, that a lawful

Overworld'll be considerably less shiny for guys like you and me. We make our gems off conflict—paid out from whichever side holds the upper hand."

"Conflict *does* generate advantage," Jools agreed. "That's not to say we can't make an honest living in a more equitable Overworld."

"Honest? You ain't lightin' my fire, Private."

"Adequate, then. And yes, I know that *adequate* is never enough for you. Why *did* you join the cavalry, then?" He snapped his light-brown eyes open and shut a few times.

"Same reason as you. Man's gotta keep dirt under his feet—not the other way around."

Jools also was not used to reaching an accord with the battalion's sergeant at arms. But Turner was right. They had both joined up with Rob's Battalion Zero when the griefer alliance threatened to eliminate their way of life—selling their services to the highest bidder on a contract basis. To Jools's mind, his freelance career had afforded him the greatest amount of personal freedom. He'd enjoyed plenty of time off, he always had work when he wanted it, and he never had to take permanent sides. This stint with the cavalry was a temporary position until he could resume freelancing.

*Those were the days,* Jools thought. Before the griefer bosses tied up the biome boundaries in an attempt to dominate the Overworld, the self-described detail consultant had ridden his palomino stallion, Beckett, wherever the winds of fortune blew. If the crime syndicate needed a way to siphon funds from a building project, Jools was there. If builders wanted to protect their construction site from thieves, ditto. The reputation of employers didn't matter—only devising the perfect scenario to achieve the desired outcome. As long as the young strategist stayed outside of their ranks, legal and moral consequences couldn't touch him.

But once the griefers used enchanted mobs to restrict travel, Jools's freewheeling career stalled. Biome borders became battle zones. His cavalry mates, Turner and Stormie, who also made their gems on a contract basis, encountered the same trouble. So when they met by chance, it had seemed only natural to join forces with Rob and the others to restore the natural balance of free enterprise, along with a just government that would protect it. They were still working on those goals.

Jools's old urge to remain unaffiliated seemed to be slipping, though, and he suspected that Turner and Stormie felt the same way. Having fought together against the Griefer Imperial Army, the once-solo players now felt a certain allegiance to one another—and even to the fledgling United Biomes of the Overworld.

After all, if the greater good didn't conquer the rising tide of evil, they'd all be enslaved and penniless.

"I do prefer building my own fortune to adding to Dr. Dirt's or Lady Craven's . . . or Termite's," Jools admitted. "And in order to make a living, one does need to remain alive."

"Or, at least, to respawn next to his loot," Turner concluded.

Jools threw him a searching look. "So, you've changed your spawn point, then?"

Turner drew back. "Didn't say I did." He drummed his fingers on his knees. "Might. Mebbe after a little house-sitting job I got planned. I'ma take some . . . personal time. After my plan works out tonight."

"*Your* plan?" Jools raised his eyebrows. "You may have outlined it, but I refined it. Not to mention helming the minecart transit project, without which there would be no plan. Ergo, as a wholly new entity dependent on my brainwork, the strategy is mine."

Turner grunted, tilting his buzz-cut head at the sky. "Gettin' dark. If we don't head off those mobs, won't matter who came up with the scheme, Private." He rose and dusted off his hands, flashing the 3-D mountains tattooed across his knuckles. "Time for some thrilling heroics."

Turner was bound for a silverfish massacre, while Jools was to play a different role in thwarting the latest griefer plot. The quartermaster didn't mind missing a melee with dangerous arthropods. He preferred any battle he could win without drawing a blade.

"Carry on, then, Sergeant," Jools said dismissively to his superior, getting to his feet as well. "I'm off to declare Beta a zombie-free zone."

It would be the last time he'd consider victory an all-or-none prospect.

\*

Jools watched Turner, Captain Rob, and the battalion's scout, Frida, set off for the city of Beta to fulfill their mission. Then the quartermaster opened the company inventory and doled out some gunpowder charges to Stormie, their artilleryman, and a few stacks of carrots to Kim, the cavalry master of horses.

"Wish I could stick around to watch your pony show, love," he said to Kim, who had donned her best pink parade armor to wow the assembled crowd of villagers. Tiny Kim rode the tallest horse in the cavalry, and was known to put on an exciting program of trick riding. She would make a striking ringmaster—her armor matched her pink skin. Her black eyes matched her shiny, black hair, which peeked out from under the dyed helmet, along with a single golden earring.

She thanked Jools for the carrots on the horses'
behalf. "You make sure that train full of zombies
switches back on Lady Craven," she said fiercely.
"Then I'll put on a whole circus just for you."

Kim never shrank from danger herself. Jools
thought she had the greatest proportion of courage to
her size of anyone he knew—other than Grimley, his
auntie's Chihuahua, back in his old life. He glanced at
Stormie, a well-known adventurer and the battalion's
artillery expert. Her skin was the color of gathering
storm clouds, and her curly, black ponytail cascaded
over her black crop top and ended at her shorts. She
added some of the gunpowder Jools gave her to the
paper and firework stars she was using to craft rockets.
Grimley's bark and bite combined would be no match
for Stormie's explosive skill set.

"Reckon you'll be able to see *my* show from your
control tower," she said to Jools. "Just look up."

The circus act and fireworks display would be fronts
for the battalion's real objective—a bold response to
the griefer plot that their captain had recently uncov-
ered. The battalion had learned that, in an effort to
destroy the new UBO capital city and the unified government it would house, enchanted mobs had been
sent by minecart to kill whomever the bomb did not.

Jools would never have entangled himself in such a
conflict before he'd met up with Kim, Stormie, Turner,

and company, but lending them his trust had been worth it. It felt good to have such capable warriors at his back. He hadn't died since he'd joined the cavalry.

Jools checked the time. "Right, mates. Inside an hour, this'll all be over." He touched Stormie's arm and grinned. "Send up a purple glitter rocket for me." With that, he turned on his heel and headed for the minecart yard.

The roundhouse was empty when he arrived. The rails that entered and exited the turnaround would remain idle, thanks to the U-shaped track that Jools's minecart crew had laid south of town. When the mob-laden train of carts topped the extreme hills, bound for the city, the new rails would shoot them right back the way they'd come. *Take that, Lady Craven,* Jools thought, hoping the griefer queen was, indeed, the one behind the evil ploy. The quartermaster had taken great pleasure in switching her game mode during their last encounter. Perhaps another crushing defeat would render her AFK for good.

He took the steps of the control tower two at a time. All that remained to do was capture Lady Craven's lackey, Termite, when he showed up to welcome his undead troops. In his mind, Jools pictured the two-legged pest: pear-shaped body, pointy limbs, bulging eyes, and perhaps, two antennae sticking out of his head. "A real creepy-crawly," he said to himself.

As Jools neared the top of the tower from which he'd rigged a suffocation sand trap, he heard a sound behind him on the steps. "Steve?" he called, thinking one of the minecart crew had interrupted his R and R to follow him.

In answer, he heard a *click*. Jools froze on the top step. His mind raced.

*Immobilized on pressure plate. Footsteps approaching. Kim: entering center ring. Stormie: on far hillside. Turner, Rob, Frida: out of range in city caverns.*

He rolled his eyes downward, careful not to move.

*Gold material . . . weighted pressure plate. Might activate weapons or explosives. Might not. Footsteps: closer!*

A wave of music and laughter drifted up from the festival below.

*No one to hear me yell; no one paying attention, anyhow. Horses, armor, potions—all back in camp.*

Now a wave of nausea swept over him. "Best laid plans . . ." he murmured.

"—are meant to be spoiled" came a quiet voice behind him.

Jools nearly jumped out of his skin, but remembered to keep his feet glued to the floor at the last second.

*"Hyeh, hyeh, hyeh . . ."*

The papery laugh seemed to push all the air out of the tiny tower cubicle. Jools gasped for breath. The hair on his neck stood on end.

"You thought you could fool me," his captor said in a calm voice drenched with bad intent. "But I am not here to wait for the night train with you. I already know what you've done to the tracks."

*Termite!* Jools's rigid body went clammy with cold sweat. "How could *I* mean to fool you? I don't even know who you are."

He felt something hard poke him in the back.

"You lie. You all know my name. Just as I know yours . . . Julian, the third."

Again, he jumped, this time as if his damp hand had grasped a live redstone wire. *How can he know that Dad's dad was named Julian?* If there was one thing Jools feared, it was someone knowing more than he did. Or knowing as much when they shouldn't.

He did what he usually did when faced with an overwhelming mental challenge. He bluffed.

"My mates'll be onto you by now. Have you *seen* Stormie and Turner? 'Tough' and 'Tougher.' They'll make mincemeat of you."

"Your mercenary is already out of ammunition," the griefer boss said evenly. "And your artilleryman soon will be."

Jools tried his best to sound unworried. "Leaving the better part of our army on the warpath. They'll find us. You do realize there's only one way out of this tower."

"For me, perhaps. Why not take a step and find yourself . . . another route?"

*Bomb!* was all Jools's brain could scream.

"Or don't. Frankly, I couldn't be bothered with the wiring on that. It's not hooked up to anything. I just wanted to frighten you."

*Counterbluff? Truth? Big, fat, smelly lie?* Jools didn't know whether to move or not. His knees were so weak that he wouldn't have a choice for much longer.

He felt the poking in his back again, but this time it was sharper. He trembled.

"Looks like it worked. *Hyeh, hyeh, hyeh* . . . Now, turn around easy and lead me back down this staircase."

The unseen blade broke skin, and Jools's knees gave way. He stumbled forward, then back. When he caught his balance, he twisted around to see a dark-haired woman pointing a gold sword at his rib cage. She wore white, plastic-rimmed glasses that magnified her dark eyes. Her expression was almost serene, except for a tinge of unmerited satisfaction—the kind of glee a shoplifter might feel when waving good-bye to the store greeter.

"*You're* Termite?" Jools blurted out. She poked him with the sword in answer, and he began slowly descending the steps. *She's a "she"! Not a "he" or an "it." How could I have made such a wrong assumption?* Jools scrambled to sound nonchalant. "Your reputation precedes you."

"Why? What have you heard?"

Jools thought of all the grief this insect had already caused: stealing building supplies, damaging property, threatening lives. "What have I heard? That you're the kind of vermin that wants fumigating." He stopped short several steps from the bottom, crouched down, and leaned backward, trying to take Termite by surprise and trip her.

Nothing happened.

He twisted his head to look, but she had already deftly leapt over him and stood at the tower base when he turned back. The swift move sent his mind into overdrive: *Save myself, save my friends! Must get to the door. . . .*

"Remember this, my pet," Termite said, returning to her position behind Jools and prodding him to exit the control tower. "There is one person in the Overworld who knows what you're going to do before you do it. So, before you tug that rope to activate the sand trap, I'll tell you who that person is. It's me."

Termite's sword butt met Jools's skull in a swift good-night kiss.

# CHAPTER 2

ONE MONTH LATER

JOOLS REELED IN HIS FISHING LINE, REMOVED A bone, and cast the hook back into the lake.

"Bone? Probability: twelve percent. Next up, I predict . . . hmm." He knit his brow. "Water bottle."

His friend and commanding officer, Roberto, wriggled his bare toes in the water chunks that lapped against the shore. "Why don't you just enchant your rod, Quartermaster?"

"For a slight increase in the chance of treasure?" Jools scoffed. "Practicing my forecasts is much more valuable." His bobber dipped, and he reeled in the line again. "Water bottle! I can always use another for my brewing stand." He put the item aside and typed a figure into the laptop computer that sat open next to him. "What did I tell you? Probability—"

"I know, I know," said Rob impatiently. "You're a hundred percent right. Look, Jools, we're supposed to be on vacation. Can't you just relax?"

Jools narrowed his eyes at the captain. "Rhetorical question?"

"No. That's an order." Rob got to his feet. "After all we went through last month, taking some time off is a—"

"I know," Jools broke in. "A mandatory request."

They both winced. Rob had issued another ultimatum a while back that hadn't worked out quite as he'd predicted.

*Who could blame him?* Jools knew the cowboy-turned-cavalry commander was still working the bugs out of his program. He'd been thrust into the role of leader as a complete newcomer to the game. Rather than chafe against the young man's control, Jools had embraced it. He certainly didn't want the job. And the other members of Battalion Zero were far too self-absorbed to bring the unit together. *Who could blame them?* That's what Survival mode was all about.

So, Jools typically obeyed Rob's wishes, for the good of the group. He couldn't change his fundamental nature, though. "Dreadfully sorry, mate. This is how I fish." He typed something else into his spreadsheet and cast out his line once more. "Next up, I predict: fish."

"That's a long shot," Rob said wryly.

"Actually, fairly common, at sixty percent odds."

"You know, Quartermaster, there's more to life than facts and figures. Take girls, for example. When's the last time you went on a date?"

*A date? Well, there was that school dance I almost went to . . . or the time Jaspreet and I almost went to the movies alone, but Whit tagged along . . .* "When's the last time *you* went on a date, Captain?"

Rob colored. "Fraternizing with troops and villagers is . . . discouraged in the cavalry manual." He sighed and tugged his cowboy boots back onto his air-dried feet. "I'm gonna go rustle up some grub," he said. "Do me a favor. Try to take it easy. Go for a hike, or something."

"Yes, sir," Jools said, fiddling with his laptop. "I'll try."

The captain wandered off toward their base camp.

When something struck the bobber again, Jools reeled in a fish. Bored with the easy game, he abandoned his rod and computer, and set off for a walk around the lake.

The blue pool lay in a red clay bowl surrounded by a spiral of tall rock formations. The two cavalry mates had ridden away from their station at the capital city of Beta to their old hideout in Bryce Mesa—an area of high desert naturally protected by rings of striped

rock towers and spiny cacti. Rob had suggested vaca-
tioning here, at the site of one of Battalion Zero's early
victories against the griefer army. He thought it might
take the sting out of their recent run-in with Termite.
The captain and the company vanguard, Frida, were
the only ones who'd survived it.

Jools had to admit the scenery was soothing after
the stress of respawning. The clay mesa ground looked
so spic-and-span, with a few bare-limbed bushes and
trickling blue creeks to break up the expanse. Rock
stair-steps climbed above the flat valley floor to meet
dramatic sandstone hoodoos—tall spires that seemed
to watch over travelers who passed by. The silver and
orange hoodoos, green cacti, and lapis-colored waters
lent vivid color to the postcard scene. But as soon as
the quartermaster acknowledged the splendor of these
surroundings, his mind shifted back to work. All he
could think about were the many tasks left undone
back at cavalry headquarters in Beta.

"Dying was not on my to-do list," he murmured.
Creating an Overworld rail system was at the top of it.

He had pinched his transit crew—the six "Thunder
Boys"—from a minecart gang that had been plagu-
ing an ice plains village. After a brief training period,
they had completed phase one of the rail project, and
were about to begin phase two. Under Jools's direction they had connected a dual loop of track between

Beta, Sunflower, and Spike City—the first settlements to join the new unified biome alliance. This linked the Overworld's central extreme hills with the sunflower plains in the northern hemisphere and the ice plains in the southern hemisphere. Jools was extremely proud of this accomplishment. But travel remained crude, at best. Phase two would posh it all up, with proper rail stations, set schedules, and parlor cars that ore workers would scarcely recognize as minecarts.

"Now, that's what I'd call civilized," he said to himself. He'd taken to the project with a passion, intrigued with transforming lawless gangsters into much-needed transit police. While he'd brought the six scofflaws a long way, he felt less than comfortable leaving them unsupervised for any length of time. If Rob hadn't practically kidnapped him and taken him on this camping trip, he'd be keeping an eagle eye on them right now.

Jools's stomach grumbled. *Should've eaten that raw fish,* he thought. Then he remembered that Rob might be cooking steaks over an open fire. He retraced his steps, retrieved his fishing equipment and loot, and headed back to camp.

While still a hundred blocks off, though, he heard hoof beats and then saw two riders coming his way. He pulled an iron sword from his inventory and stood his ground. Two stout horses—a smallish black-and-white paint, and a taller bay warmblood—brought their riders swiftly toward him.

"Jools!" came a familiar voice. Stormie rode the smaller mount, and Kim galloped up on the giant. The young women were dressed for the trail in tall boots and clingy riding shirts and pants. Stormie's were basic black and Kim's, her signature pink. The pair skidded to a stop. "Where's the captain?" Stormie called.

"We have news!" Kim said.

Jools felt his blood surge. "Thank the mods! I was halfway mad from all this peace and quiet."

Kim jumped down from her stallion, Nightwind, and gave Jools a leg up behind the saddle. "Rob's going to want to hear this," she said, mounting and gathering the reins again. "We had to cut our beach trip short. Something crazy happened to the eastern ocean."

"Isn't that where Lady Craven was said to be hiding out?" Jools asked, bouncing a bit on Nightwind's rump.

"Could be she's behind the trouble," Stormie said, urging her horse, Armor, alongside them.

"Trouble?" Jools said. "This vacation might turn out better than I thought."

*

The three friends found their captain lounging by the campfire in his chaps, jeans, vest, and western shirt, an empty plate beside him. He'd set up a row of water bottles a few blocks off and was tossing rocks at them for target practice.

*Ting! Ting! Tong . . . crash!* He hit three in a row, knocking them all over and breaking the last bottle.

"Nice one," Jools said as the horses slowed from a trot to halt before the cavalry commander. Whinnies of greeting came from Beckett and Rob's black Morgan horse, Saber, who were tied to a spider-string picket line.

Rob paused his stone throwing. "Corporal! Artilleryman! What are you girls doing out here?"

Stormie vaulted off of Armor. "Looking for you, sir."

"Tired of beach combing?" Rob asked.

Kim let Jools slide down first, and then she dismounted. "We might have a situation, Captain."

Rob tossed another rock and missed his target. "Let me guess. Sunburn?"

"Seriously, sir." Stormie's dark eyes clouded. "Possible griefer army activity in the east."

"Goody, goody gumdrops," Jools murmured wholeheartedly.

Rob looked less thrilled, but was now all ears. "Report, please." He let them tie up their horses, then passed around some leftover steaks.

Between bites, Kim and Stormie told Rob and Jools about their beach trail ride, which had been more disturbing than rejuvenating.

"We were riding north, up the coast of cold beach," Stormie said.

"We made a snow shelter and turned in for the night," Kim added. "When we woke up the next day, the beach was . . . bigger."

Rob cocked his head at Jools, who leaned forward intently.

"The sand blocks extended out in the ocean farther than we remembered, anyhow," Stormie said. "Thought we was just seein' things, or maybe had too much flower water the night before. But the same thing happened the next night, at a camp up the beach."

"Are you sure the tide wasn't just coming in?" Rob asked.

"Tide? I've seen that mod once," Jools said. "Makes waves. Was that it?"

Stormie eyed Kim, who shrugged.

Jools persisted. "Come on. Waves move. They undulate." He demonstrated a rolling wave with his hand. "Could it have been a tide mod?"

Stormie shook her head. "It was more like somebody had replaced chunks of ocean with chunks of sand."

Jools thought harder. "Or . . . could be they *removed* ocean chunks to reveal what lies beneath them."

"You say this happened twice?" Rob asked.

Kim nodded. "Twice like that. The third night it was gravel."

Jools dropped the remainder of his steak and jumped to his feet. "I sense a pattern forming. We must investigate!"

"We must tell the judge and colonel first," Rob countered, referring to the UBO administrators.

Jools screwed up his face in annoyance. "They're not our nannies. And we're on holiday. I say we break camp and ride out to the sea."

"With hardly any concrete information, no armor, and no backup?" Rob stared him down. "This sounds big. We're going to need full ranks."

Jools threw up his hands. "Good luck with that, then. We're one vanguard and one weapons expert short," he said sharply. Frida was on leave, and Turner was . . . wherever Turner was.

Rob didn't respond right away. He and Jools had skirted the subject of the missing sergeant at arms since leaving the city. After the bomb went off, Rob and Frida had fled to safety, seeing to the villagers and horses in Beta. Jools, Stormie, and Kim had respawned soon afterward, but Turner was nowhere to be found. Since this behavior wasn't unusual for him, nobody worried. At first.

Days had passed. The settlers moved into the city and set up a volunteer guard, and still the sergeant hadn't reappeared. He'd left his horse, Duff, safely behind with the rest of the herd. Now, the cavalry mates feared the worst—that either death or dishonesty had parted them from Turner for good.

Judge Tome suggested the battalion take some well-deserved time off to recuperate. When leave was announced, Vanguard Frida had lit out for the jungle—alone. The commander and the quartermaster chose to camp at Bryce Mesa, while the horse master and artilleryman headed for the beach. Sergeant Turner hadn't been present to be dismissed.

Now Jools recalled the last time he'd seen the sergeant at arms, the night they'd all ended up in Termite's underground bunker. The griefer's plan to exterminate first the battalion members, then the villagers, and—by default—the biome unification effort, had almost succeeded. Trapped in a bomb-rigged room deep inside the city caverns, the troopers had selected Rob and Frida to escape with their lives during the fuse delay. The others—including Jools—had agreed to die, hoping to avoid maximum damage and respawn at their bedsides in cavalry camp. Everyone had—except for Turner.

"Well," Rob said, finally, "we'll need to recall Frida, at least."

"How?" Stormie asked. "Turner was the only person who knew her clan coordinates."

To his surprise, Jools wished the opposite were true—that Frida could tell them where Turner was. "Where could the big lug have gone?" he asked, knowing no one could answer. Nobody said so, but none of the options were good. Either Turner had taken too much damage during the blast—making it impossible for him to respawn in his familiar form—or he'd lied about synchronizing his spawn point with the others'.

In any case, Turner wasn't available to hunt down their scout, and Rob wasn't brash—or foolhardy—enough to send a splintered battalion into unknown danger.

Rob pressed his lips together, considering their prospects. "Our intel places Lady Craven somewhere in the vicinity of the eastern ocean. The tracks that Frida found after the explosion suggest that Termite headed that way, as well."

"We thought it all added up to more than coincidence, sir," Kim said.

"Even I'd hate to meet up with those griefers without Meat on our team," Stormie said sadly, using Frida's pet name for Turner. "I sure hope he didn't leave the game."

Rob wasn't feeling so charitable. "For my money, he probably lied to us. If he didn't change his spawn point—the way he said he did—then he'd reenter play wherever he took his last big licking. He might've thrown in with the syndicate. Bluedog and Rafe would be glad to give him work, for a cut of the profits."

"Yes," Jools agreed, in light of the sergeant's tendency toward deception and self-preservation. "It's quite possible he'd take up with those moneygrubbing lowlifes. Perhaps we should set out a bowl of emeralds at suppertime and see if he comes running."

The girls began to protest when Jools shushed them. *Bowl of emeralds . . . bowl of emeralds . . .* "Hello? That's it!" His eyes lit up. "I'll wager Sergeant Turner's *not* permanently dead or unrecognizably maimed," Jools went on. "He probably *didn't* give up on us and go AWOL, either. And . . . he might even have been telling the truth when he said he'd matched his spawn point with ours."

"What makes you think so?" Rob pressed him.

"It was something he said right before the Termite episode. And awhile back—on one of our trips to the Nether." Jools paused dramatically. "He's on a job, mates! I'd stake my paycheck on it."

# CHAPTER 3

"WOULD IT HAVE KILLED THE GUY TO LEAVE A note?" Rob complained after Jools had shared his hypothesis on Turner's whereabouts.

Jools regarded the captain with amusement. "Did you ever see Sergeant Turner pick up a pen? Or a book, for that matter?"

Rob ducked his head. "Not everyone has as complete a command of the English language as you do, Quartermaster."

"Be that as it may. I think you'll agree that Turner hasn't enough consideration for those who care about him to ease their minds with a simple, 'Gone to lunch—be back soon.'"

Stormie clucked. "He might not be that cold-hearted. Maybe it's a self-image thing. Or maybe he didn't think we'd care."

"I guess we could've been . . . sweeter to him," Kim said slowly.

Rob snorted. "What goes around, comes around."

Jools said nothing. He recognized Turner's bluster for what it was: a defense mechanism. He and the mercenary were far more alike than he wanted to admit.

Rob, knowing he couldn't do without the sergeant's help right now, accepted the inevitable. "Are we going where I think we're going, Quartermaster?"

A grin crept across Jools's pale face. "A certain Nether fortress, I believe." He turned to Stormie. "If you collect the obsidian and ignition, I'll look up the coordinates."

*I do love solving a cipher,* Jools thought to himself. He'd figured out that Turner *had* lied: to him, when he'd denied changing his spawn point that day in the stable yard. He'd only copped to it in a moment of weakness, later that night when he realized he'd never leave Termite's bunker alive. It had been a point of pride with the mercenary to keep his origins secret. But Rob had rightfully asked the troopers to sync their spawn points to cavalry camp, to protect their mission. Even Turner couldn't argue with that objective. The revelation that he'd finally followed the order had certainly shocked everyone.

So, maybe Turner felt his reputation was tarnished, once the others knew he wasn't as Teflon as he'd made out. These little disappearing acts of his served to throw the spotlight back on his unpredictability . . . which always made him seem a bit more fearsome. The last time he'd taken unauthorized leave, he'd suffered a court-martial—but there was no guarantee he wouldn't retaliate, or vanish again. This time, Turner must have respawned in camp but departed immediately.

*"When this is all over . . . when this is all over . . ."* The snippet of conversation drifted back to Jools. Turner had planned to take some "personal time," somewhere. House-sitting, he'd said. Jools didn't think he'd left the game.

All it took to determine the sergeant's destination was to recall another coincidental absence: Colonel M's. The First War veteran had retreated to his home in the Nether when Termite threatened wide-scale destruction. Epic battle wounds had prevented him from respawning intact, leaving him as just a large, disembodied head. Any further damage . . . Any further damage might wipe the old ghost out completely. He'd left Judge Tome in charge of city affairs until he returned. *Until he returned* . . . When Colonel M came back, he'd need a house sitter! He had generously donated his iron golems to the new city. A fellow couldn't leave his personal Nether fortress unoccupied and unguarded forever.

Jools knew the colonel had been seeking a caretaker for some time. Considering the fortress was full of wither skeletons and that the Nether wasn't exactly Shangri-la, he hadn't had much luck. "Only one person I know would take that job," Jools said to himself as he looked up the colonel's coordinates on his computer. He silently thanked the mercenary for being so true to form.

\*

*If I were world programmer,* Jools decided, *I'd hand out, rather than take away, experience points for dying. I think I'm getting better at it.* True, he mourned no loss of life so much as his own. However, he'd noticed that this most recent purchase of "The Farm" hurt less than his previous deaths—psychologically, not physically. In fact, it had been a positive experience, other than the sudden drop in XP. Thanks to Battalion Zero, Jools not only regained his own inventory when he respawned, he still held the keys to the company stores. It was the uncertainty over how much he'd lose that'd made death so unattractive in the past.

"Is it overly morbid to think about dying en route to the Nether?" Jools asked from his perch in Beckett's saddle. Before them, Stormie guided Armor alongside the minecart tracks, toward the Nether portal they'd placed. Behind him, Kim and Rob brought up the rear file on Nightwind and Saber.

"My answer?" Kim said. "Yes. Keep any dark thoughts to yourself. It's gloomy enough down there."

"Better to visit the underworld while we're livin' than for all eternity," Stormie supposed.

"Nobody's dying," Rob said flatly. "We've done this before, we can do it again. Besides, Jools, Beckett's jumping has improved."

Jools chuckled. The last time they'd visited Colonel M, Beckett had refused to jump a lava flow until Saber gave him a lead over it. "Now that we have the exact coordinates," Jools said, "we can take the express lane, anyway."

As he said this, three souped-up minecarts flew past in a blur of hot pink, purple, and green. The horseback riders barely glimpsed the leather-clad drivers who shouted unintelligible greetings.

As they whizzed by, the horses danced, but remained under control. Then three more modified vehicles approached from behind and passed the group more slowly. Each of the drivers was dressed identically in black jumpsuits and wore mirrored sunglasses that hid their eyes. It was easy to see why Jools hadn't been able to tell them apart when they'd first taken the job on the transit line.

"Steve!" he called. "And Steve, and Steve!" Unable to speak their dialect, the quartermaster had simply given them all the same name. "Tell those other fellows to slow down! We'll be back with some prismarine for the station facades before you can say *bōsōzoku.*"

The three Steves broadcast modified engine sounds, pumped their fists, and gunned the carts after their mates. "Those boys are incorrigible," Jools pronounced, both irked and pleased. The once-unruly minecart gang members were managing to take orders and patrol the vulnerable rail system . . . but they still liked to play.

In a short time, the horses reached the gateway Stormie had crafted, and their riders dismounted. They'd have to lead the mounts through the portal. Once down under, the sure-footed beasts would traverse the netherrack terrain much more easily than the troopers could on their own. Still, anything might happen down there. Jools gritted his teeth as he and Beckett stepped into the mist of purple particles and through to the next plane.

The underworld was as he remembered—less a fiery vista than a mix of sensations: sharp, hot, and dim. They all stood for a few moments, trying to get their bearings. "The timeless beauty of the Nether," Jools remarked sarcastically.

Yet, there was something beautiful about the environment on its own terms. Each element of the landscape seemed to dovetail with the next. Lava pools, streams, and falls provided relief from the seemingly endless serrated terraces of iron-hard netherrack. Clusters of glowstone and random patches of fire gave off just enough light to reveal how perfectly black the darkness was.

Still, the best thing about a trip to the Nether was knowing you could leave. "It's a nice place to visit, but I wouldn't want to pitch a tent here," Jools said, voicing everyone's thoughts.

They were planning on a swift visit to the fortress and a quick retreat, so they didn't bother fortifying the portal. Colonel M's special arrangement with the local hostiles meant that a fallback shelter wouldn't be necessary, either. The colonel's underworld home lay just on the other side of an inky chasm. Without a natural bridge, they'd have to pick their way down, up, and back again. They mounted the horses and set off on the short, yet hazardous, ride.

"Keep a sharp eye there, Artilleryman," Rob called.

"Sharp as netherrack, sir," Stormie answered.

Again Jools contemplated the safety that came with the company of friends, two- and four-legged. He patted Beckett's pale gold neck, just as a rogue fire sparked at his feet. Level-headed Beckett merely stepped around the flames.

Armor stopped at the edge of the abyss. "I can't see the bottom, Captain," Stormie said.

Jools carefully crept down from the stirrups. "Allow me. Night vision draughts for everyone." He passed out the potions and downed his own ration.

Instantly, the view became clearer. As they moved the horses forward again, Jools could see nothing in the hole but blackish netherrack blocks and trenches. *Funny how "the unknown" is sometimes just "the known" plus a healthy dose of fear, nothing more.*

Suddenly, Stormie cried out.

"What is it?" Rob yelled, unable to see her from his place in line. He reined Saber off to the side.

"Armor stepped on a magma cube! Its eyes must've been closed. That made it perfectly camouflaged!" Before Jools could react, Stormie had pulled her sword and hacked at the square mobster.

The demon split into four smaller versions of itself, all of which began hopping toward the riders.

"Don't move!" Kim called. "They might run you into a ditch!"

"She's right," Jools confirmed. "Wait till they jump at you. Then hit them when they're in the air!"

Rob took over. "Battalion, ready!" Each of the four mini cubes bounded toward a player. "Attack!"

With precision timing, the four troopers raised and wielded their iron swords. But when the blades met their targets, the magma cubes split again, each producing four more, even tinier, hostile blocks. Jools wouldn't have paid them any mind if not for the sixteen pairs of coal-lit eyes that hinted at the mobsters' deadly lava cores.

"Troops: again!" Rob called. "Ready . . . attack! Attack! Attack! Attack!"

*Training's paid off,* Jools thought, as he wiped his sword on his jacket sleeve and put his weapon away. Then he climbed down to gather the magma cream drops for his brewing inventory.

The riders moved through the darkened gorge without further incident. Soon, the shadowy outline of Colonel M's fortress appeared up ahead. A pair of torches framed the gate.

"Cheery, innit?" Jools quipped as they dismounted. He led Beckett forward and rang the redstone doorbell.

For a very long moment, all they could hear from inside was the nerve-racking sound of bone hitting metal, and the odd fireball gust. Then the brick gate opened a crack, and more torchlight showed through the smoky haze filtering out. A distinctive gruff voice issued a butler's greeting: "Who shall I say is here?"

\*

In his sweetest girlie voice, Jools answered, "Avon calling!"

The gate opened wider. There, in his customary cargo pants, ripped T-shirt, and combat boots stood Turner. The mercenary's eyes widened when he saw his friends. "Well, I'll be a—"

"You'll be confined to quarters, is what you'll be," said Rob, hustling past Jools to confront the absentee sergeant.

"These *is* my new temporary quarters," Turner insisted stubbornly. "No one ever said I couldn't take a side job in between death-defying missions."

"You could've let us know," Rob snapped.

Stormie dropped Armor's reins and ran up to give Turner a hug. "Glad to see you, Meat," she said.

"We feared the worst," Kim announced, moving close enough to squeeze Turner affectionately on his mesa biome tattoo.

He tried to cover his pleasure and embarrassment. "Aw, ya can't kill a pro. . . ."

"Not true," Jools said. "Probability of death hovers above fifty-fifty in Survival mode. Also, if you're a *pro*, I'm a monkey's uncle."

Turner blinked at him, then opened his mouth to object. The approach of an enormous, disembodied head from within the fortress, however, distracted him.

"You are, unwittingly, quite right, Quartermaster," the head boomed in a stately voice. "You and your fully human kind are closely related to primates. And I am attempting to groom Sergeant Turner as a professional manservant."

"*Servant?*" Turner echoed. "Thought I was paid management material."

"Personal service does not preclude pay," Colonel M said, his wild bush of gray hair bouncing with emphasis. "Poor service does. Now, are you going to usher our guests inside?"

Jools took great satisfaction in watching Turner make way for the travelers and see to their horses. Meanwhile, Colonel M nodded them in the direction of a conversation area, where several large, subdued magma cubes served as seating, with smaller magma cubes serving as footrests. After their short, but tense, journey, the four troopers were glad to take a load off in a secure space.

The fortress was protected, thanks to Colonel M's security system—a platoon of undead wither skeletons that clamored behind an iron grating in the next room. At the colonel's command, they would battle any unwelcome intruders to the death. Jools was relieved to know that Battalion Zero's members were considered friends, not foes.

"It is good to see that you four survived," Colonel M said to Rob and company.

"You look well," Rob complimented him. The colonel's face showed good color, like highly polished saddle leather, and his dark eyes were bright.

"The long rest has done me some good," he admitted. "Now, where is our favorite vanguard?"

"Frida's on leave," the cavalry commander replied.

"I hope this visit doesn't represent urgent business."

"Well, sir, it does, and it doesn't. The city of Beta isn't at risk—yet. Judge Tome sends his regards and says you can take the time you need to get your place in order before returning to work. It's Turner we've come for."

Jools added, "Yes, I'm afraid we must borrow your butler."

"Already?" Turner butted into the conversation, indignant. "I was just gettin' comfy here."

"Now, now," Stormie said. "We need you, Sarge. Kim and I ran into some . . . trouble on our trail ride."

Turner puffed up. "An' you want me to make it all better?"

Jools shot him down. "Not quite." He didn't mention that they'd come to rely on the weapons expert's defensive skills. "We just want you to find Frida so she can work her usual magic."

"Frida?" Turner shot Rob a glance. "I thought she'd escaped with you, Newbie. If you let anything happen to her . . ."

"It's 'Captain.' And you're the one who deserted her, Sergeant," Rob accused.

"Vanguard Frida is, perhaps, the most competent at survival among your ranks," Colonel M pointed out.

"She can take care of herself," Jools agreed. "When she was offered leave, she opted to spend it alone in the jungle."

"Typical," Turner muttered.

"You're the only one of us who has access to her coordinates," Rob admitted grudgingly. "We need to find her, ASAP."

Kim and Stormie filled the sergeant and colonel in on their ocean discovery and its possible implications. Then the group pieced together the events directly following the cataclysm several weeks before.

Rob said, "After we left you, Frida and I went back to cav camp to make sure the settlers were safe."

A wave of immigrants had descended on the new city before dwellings could be built, so they'd been housed in tents near Battalion Zero's encampment. They were on the verge of moving into Beta when the inauguration festivities were cut short by Termite's threats. It turned out that the griefer boss was more focused on harming the Beta project than its residents.

Jools addressed Turner. "The rest of us respawned not long after the cave walls came tumbling down. We reconvened at the bunkhouse." He waved a hand dismissively. "In the confusion, we somehow overlooked your absence."

"Wasn't *absent*," Turner grumbled. "By that time, I'd done been and gone. Can I help it if y'all's game lags?"

Jools took offense at the attack on his server. "We did not dawdle, if that's what you're implying. How *did* you get back to camp so fast? Perhaps you used a cheat." During a break in the skeleton's din, the last word echoed in the brick chamber.

"Them's fightin' words, Private." Turner lunged forward.

Colonel M leveled a laser-beam gaze at the sergeant, knocking him onto the ground. Then the old ghost cast a disapproving stare at the quartermaster. "Regardless of your intended subject's record in other arenas," the colonel said, "*no one* in this battalion cheats in Survival mode. Of that, I am certain."

After a pause, Jools said, "I do apologize. You're right, Colonel. Not even Meat, here, would do that. And I'm sure he would never strike a superior officer."

Turner picked himself up from the ground and dusted off his cargo pants. "Apology accepted. Wait a second . . ." He eyed his rival. "You got promoted?"

Jools glanced at his fingernails modestly. "Affirmative. To first lieutenant," he said, pronouncing it *lef-tenant*. "For my efforts in the transit project." While Turner grappled with the news, Kim tried to understand how the respawning troopers had missed each other. "So, Turner, I don't get it. You're saying you got back to camp before the rest of us. How come you didn't wait around?"

"Yeah, Meat," Stormie said. "Didn't you want to see if we all made it back into the game? We sure were worried about you."

"Well, I—knew you'd all land on your feet," he mumbled. "Besides, I had a line on this here house-sittin' gig, and the early bird, ya know . . ."

". . . has much in common with the worm," Jools finished for him. Then he brightened. "I told you lot he'd be on a gem hunt." He shook his head at Turner. "You're not the most complicated individual in the Overworld to figure out."

Turner sniffed and hiked a thumb at his ripped T-shirt. "What ya see is what ya get, here, pal."

Rob stood up. "I'd like to continue this little dog-eat-dog game, but we've got to get going. We left an unsecured portal as our ticket to the surface." He nodded at Colonel M. "Can you spare Turner, sir?"

The colonel couldn't help but chuckle. "I think I'll manage."

# CHAPTER 4

URNER RODE NIGHTWIND, WITH KIM PERCHED behind the saddle, and dismounted with the others at the Nether portal. They stepped back into the Overworld and marched into cavalry camp, just north of the city limits, as the sun sank. Kim and Stormie led the tired mounts to the torch-lined pasture and activated the drawbridge that let them cross the protective moat. Duff, Turner's stocky gray quarter horse, whinnied loudly from his place within the rest of the herd.

"Aren't you going to answer him, Meat?" Jools asked, demonstrating a very passable nicker of his own.

Turner glared at him and then called out, "Papa's home, boy!"

At that moment, a short, stout villager dressed smartly in riding gear walked into the paddock carrying several buckets of water. Duff trotted up to the young man and arched his neck, begging for a treat. The fellow dropped his buckets, gave Duff a piece of sugar, and affectionately roughed up the hair on his neck.

"What the—?" Turner glanced at the other troopers for an explanation. Who was handling his horse, and why?

Rob slid his eyes at Jools. "Quartermaster? Why don't you introduce the sergeant to my new adjutant? I'll be in my bunk." He sidled away, clearly handing over a job he didn't want to do.

Jools gave an evil grin. "Burk!" he summoned the teenager. "Get over here. On the double!"

Burk instantly teleported their way. He stood at attention before Jools and snapped off a salute. "Adjutant Sergeant Burkhart, reporting for duty, sir!"

The villager sported a meticulous crew cut, round spectacles, and robin's-egg blue skin as smooth as a baby's bottom. He waited for instructions like a puppy waiting for a bowl of milk.

Turner's mouth fell open.

"This fresh-faced lad is our new sergeant," Jools introduced the two. "We call him Burk."

Turner found his tongue. *"Sergeant?"*

"At ease, boy," Jools said to the cadet, who shifted his position but remained at the ready. Jools explained to Turner, "Someone had to play second-in-command while you were off gallivanting through the Nether. Beta has got a new armed guard unit that needed a leader."

"Sounds like a lot of red tape," Turner said with contempt, trying to hide his distress at missing out on one job opportunity while accepting another.

"Permission to speak, Lieutenant?" Burk asked, and Jools nodded. "I know it's a big responsibility, Mr. Turner, sir. But I'm willing to learn. We've made quite a few improvements while you were absent without leave, sir."

Turner grunted. "That's 'Sergeant,' to you, pal. A real sergeant, not an adju-, adjudi- . . . Not a baby sergeant. Veteran of several bloody campaigns with this unit. And I weren't AWOL. They prob'ly didn't tell ya; I was on an extremely covert mission in the Nether."

The young soldier's eyes grew huge behind his glasses. "Welcome back, then, Sergeant." His tone grew businesslike. "You'll want to know how we run things now."

Turner cut Jools an incredulous look. "Where'd ya get this kindergartner?" He turned back to the cadet. "Think I can figure it out on my own, Dirk."

"Burk, Sergeant. And I'm a sergeant, as well."

Turner clenched his fists and lunged forward, faking the young man out. Poor Burk shrank back.

Turner drew himself up to full height. "Call ya what I want to call ya."

"*Sergeant* Burk," Jools said, "please share the duty roster with Sergeant Meat, here."

Burk ignored Turner's scowl and pulled out a clipboard. He glanced down a list. "You're to bait for zombies every evening at dusk, Sergeant."

"That's a private's chore!"

Jools stepped in. "When you left your post, you fell to the bottom of the ladder. You'll have to put in some time as a grunt to regain it. Sorry."

"This better not mean a pay cut," Turner said through his teeth.

"Fortunately for you, we still need a sergeant at arms. Your rank holds; your seniority does not."

Turner sputtered, "I'll have me a talk with the captain, then."

Jools shook his head. "You'll report to Burk, Sergeant, who will be glad to relay your thoughts to the cavalry commander."

"In my capacity as adjutant," Burk put in earnestly. "It's all by the book."

Turner raised his eyebrows. "What book?"

"The one that's going to make your life a living hell," Jools murmured. Then, to Burk, he said, "Show Mr. Turner where the zombie slop is. And make sure he follows orders. Carry on."

\*

That night, Burk and his newbie crew of guards hacked away at the mobs that Turner's bait attracted, while Kim and Stormie inspected and cleaned horse tack. After mess call, the male members of Battalion Zero convened in the bunkhouse's common room. When Turner tried to broach the subjects of rank and duty with Rob, the captain cut him short.

"Not on the table right now, Sergeant. Let's discuss our immediate plans. First, I want a status report on the Beta project. Quartermaster?"

Among his other responsibilities, Jools acted as liaison with the Beta building team. He knew the full layout of the capital city from belowground up. While the fallen sergeant was busy chumming for zombies after sunset, Jools had checked in with the brother-and-sister building team up at the jobsite. He brought out his laptop and read from his notes.

"The settlers are settled. High-rise apartments are inhabited, and most of the single-family dwellings are nearing completion," Jools announced. "Capitol building is one hundred percent finished. It now houses the admin offices and an auditorium for public forums. With basic food, water, shelter, and transit needs met, De Vries and Crash are moving forward with constructing the new UBO museum.

It's slated to open next week. They've offered to give us a preview."

Rob nodded. "Tell them we accept."

Turner frowned. "That an optional field trip? I went to a museum once, back in Baton Rouge. Real snooze fest. I'd best be headin' for the jungle instead."

"Right," mocked Jools. "Natural wonders, antique weaponry, and the most precious gems of the Overworld. Who'd want to see that?"

"Weapons? Gems, you say? That beats the usual watercolors and plaster statues. Mebbe I could make an exception this time. . . ." Turner said.

"That you will, Sergeant," Rob said. "We'll hold off until you return with Frida. But before you go, I'm calling a night training. We're all a little rusty after the time off, and we've got to be in top form to go up against griefer agitators."

An armed training held even greater appeal for the weapons expert. "Beggin' your pardon, Cap'n," he said. "My ridin' might be rusty. My swordplay ain't."

Jools remarked, "It's the other way 'round for me. But, then, sometimes a rusty blade adds just the right amount of damage." While on his backcountry ride, he had actually missed the nightly skirmishing. He would welcome some practice.

They filed out to fetch their horses, which had been taken indoors for the evening. Kim and Stormie met the men at the modest stable that De Vries had built while the battalion was away. Spartan though it was, the wooden frame of alternating spruce and acacia blocks looked smart, and the clay roof would discourage lightning damage. Jools thought the design open and airy—features he knew Beckett would appreciate, being stalled next to the gaseous mule that belonged to Judge Tome.

Both animals were happily munching hay from their mangers when he arrived. "Eat up, Beckett, old chap," he said to his horse. "We'll be kings of the drill tonight."

Before tacking up, Jools opened the company inventory and passed out a variety of swords. If trouble drew them into an underwater battle, splash potions and bows would be of little use.

"I'll take a wood or gold sword," Kim said. "Anything I can hit with those will take nearly twice as much damage when I switch to a diamond blade."

"Give me two diamond ones," Stormie said, with a wink. "They're a girl's best friend."

That left iron swords for the men. They collected them and their mounts, and trooped out to the pasture for drill.

Captain Rob announced, "Tonight's objective is speed, on and off your horse."

*The one thing Beckett has trouble with,* Jools thought. "Can I just stay off the horse, then?" he asked.

Rob shook his head. "In the ocean biome, we might have to fight dismounted. But on our way there, or on any islands we come across, mounted melees are more likely. Turner: you watch for hostiles at the perimeter while we take turns at target practice. Horse Master? Do you have the live targets?"

Kim acted as their ground crew during trainings. "Ready to go, sir!" She pointed to a large chest.

Rob called to Jools, "Lieutenant. Since you're worried about Beckett's speed, you go first."

Jools grimaced. *Why did I open my big mouth?* He got up on the palomino stallion, drew his iron sword, and waved to Kim.

She opened the chest just long enough to release one target. A tiny chunk of green slime hopped from the box. Kim ran to the sidelines, out of range with the others already at the fence.

The miniscule mobster homed in on Jools and began jumping toward him and Beckett in baby steps: *toing! toing! toing!*

"Trooper at the ready . . . and charge!" Rob cried.

Jools kept Beckett in hand. "For pity's sake, Captain! Do you really want me to charge that?"

Before Rob could answer, the slime began hopping faster, tapping out a frantic Morse code. In an instant, it was halfway across the pasture and closing in on the stalled horse and rider.

"Whoa! I mean, go! Go!" Jools kicked Beckett into a sudden canter. The horse was as surprised as Jools was, providing just the adrenaline rush to propel them both forward.

Still, on came the slime. It tried to jump on the man in the saddle—once, twice, three times. Beckett instinctively dodged the gelatinous creature, which finally found the correct trajectory on the fourth try. But, as it bounded high enough to connect with its prey, Jools waved his sword like a badminton racquet and dealt it a death blow.

"Bravo!" called Stormie.

"Nice riding!" said Kim. She climbed back inside the fence and picked up the two slimeballs that dropped. "Excellent! We'll use them to craft new lead ropes for the horses." Then she returned to the chest. "Ready, Lieutenant?"

Jools nodded. His blood was pumping now. Even Beckett was on edge.

This time, Kim released two tiny slimes before running off. Jools didn't hesitate charging. He selected one and sent Beckett at its springing form, repeating his earlier maneuver with the sword. This, though, gave the second slimelet a chance to get close enough to land two hits. But Jools didn't feel a loss of any hearts. He simply drew back his sword and sliced through the thing with another forehand swing.

Goo dripped from his sword. He was about to wipe it off on his jacket when Rob yelled, "Dismount to fight on foot! Horse Master! Now!"

Without waiting for a sign from Jools, Kim loosed twelve of the square green mobsters and fled.

Jools's feet fumbled getting out of the stirrups. He clambered heavily to the ground, dropping Beckett's reins and raising his sword.

*toing! toing! toingtoingtoingtoingtoingtoingtoing!*

There was no time to aim. It was amazing how the slimes' speed increased the closer they got. All Jools could do was wave his blade as fast as he could in their direction. Only once did it meet goosh.

Grasping for a solution, an image from his old life flitted through his mind. He was eleven, and it was his novice hard-ball cricket season. His neighborhood team faced a whiz-kid bowler. The marksman soundly took young Jools's wicket in every at-bat . . . until Jools gave up trying to make fancy bat shots. Once he switched to plain, old vertical drives, he began clobbering the ball. The crowd thundered as the rookie produced run after run, finally sending the once-mighty bowler off to the showers.

*That's it!* Jools pictured the slime blocks as round leather balls with the brand name DUKE imprinted on them in gold letters. Instantly, he changed his game from badminton to cricket. Using vertical strokes, he found he could slice one slime on the upswing and the next on the downswing. In moments, he had reduced the mob to a dozen-plus slimeballs on the ground.

At the hearty applause, he gave an exaggerated bow, and then swiped his dripping sword against his jacket sleeve with a flourish. *Best night training ever!* he thought, stoked beyond belief. *Let's see anyone do better than that.*

He relinquished the arena to Stormie, who was up next. She had the good grace to leave one of her swords on the sidelines, so as not to take an unfair advantage over Jools's performance. She needn't have worried. He had wandered off into a sweet daydream. In his mind, he was a lad again, watching the defeated bowler scuttle away in shame as he was carried off the field on his teammates shoulders.

# CHAPTER 5

LATER THAT NIGHT, WHILE JOOLS WAS DREAMING of rigging the perfect sand trap, his computer burbled loudly enough to wake him. A message was coming through on his secure server. He rubbed the imaginary sand from his eyes and fished for his laptop, which sat next to his bed. The worried face of their ice plains delegate appeared on the screen.

"Gaia! Is everything all right in Spike City?" he asked.

The genial priest must have also been awakened by news. Her long, thick black hair was mussed and woven with yesterday's roses. "Don't be alarmed, Jools. We're fine here. I've received some information—rumors, really—that I thought I should pass along without delay."

"What is it?"

She frowned. "Some of our young explorers had such a scare at the ocean edge that they came running back in the dark."

Jools sat up straighter in bed. "Let me guess: the waters are receding, being replaced with sand and gravel chunks."

Gaia drew back. "Why—yes. But how did you—?"

"Two of our troopers had the same experience." Jools felt bad for not warning the conscientious biome representative. "So sorry. We should've let you know we're pursuing the possibility of GIA activity out there."

"Do you really think the griefers could be behind it? We've had no sightings of imperial army troops, if that's any consolation."

"That's not an indicator, in itself," Jools reasoned. "Sad to say, the victories we've had over Lady Craven, Termite, and their ilk, have only driven them deeper underground."

"Or, in this case, underwater."

"Ten-four. Battalion Zero is poised to ride out and investigate shortly. We'll keep you posted," he promised.

"Very good. I apologize for the late message."

"Not at all. Your corroboration lends urgency to the mission." He thanked her and signed off.

Jools relayed the report at breakfast the next morning in the common room.

"That's good to hear," Stormie said. "Kim and I still weren't sure about what we saw." She passed around a plate of cooked eggs.

"Let's get eyes on that territory," Rob said, helping himself from the platter. "We'll clear this up. Quartermaster, prepare a mobile inventory of necessaries for an ocean survey."

"Oh, boy. A trip to the shore," Jools joked darkly. "I hope it's better than my family holidays at Crane Beach. Fights, followed by arguments, topped off with nobody speaking to each other. That was actually the best part."

"Hurt feelings might be the least of our problems," Stormie said, twisting the conversation back toward the potential danger.

"Ever been underwater, sir?" Kim asked Rob. "Guardian mobs spawn there night and day."

"I spent my first Overworld moments in the western ocean," Rob reminded her. "But I was only in the water long enough to figure out how to get out of it." He paused. "I didn't see any aquatic hostiles. You're saying there are *more* monsters I don't know about?"

"Guardians and elder guardians," Jools replied. "Were I to classify them in Latin, I'd dub them *malus* and *malus*-er. *Bad* and *Badder*. They don't despawn. They fire laser beams at you until you're dead. If they don't decimate you with their thorns first. Yes, let's all take a lovely holiday at the beach."

The cavalry commander looked queasy. He got up, tossed the rest of his breakfast into the company inventory, and slumped back down at the table. Although Rob's confidence had grown during his time with the battalion, it took time for him to get used to any new threat, Jools had noticed. He tried to reassure the captain, "Not to worry, sir. I once spent an entire player lifetime adrift in a boat. It was a short life, and I can attest, firsthand, that guardians mostly spawn in ocean monuments."

Rob looked at him. "Yeah? What are those? Underwater museums?"

Stormie answered. "They're more like jungle temples, only they generate in the deep sea. Plenty of prospects for mining or finding loot there—if you can get past the hostile mobs."

"I've seen pictures of the monuments," Kim added. "They're beautifully constructed. Like prismarine palaces."

"De Vries would love them," Jools said, referring to their builder friend. "Better not tell him we're going or he'll drop the Beta project like a hot potato."

Rob took in all this new information. "Well, sounds like we have some prep work to do. Which of us has the most firsthand experience with these biomes?"

The others looked at the famed Overworld traveler.

"Stormie?" Rob prompted. "What do we need to know?"

She thought about it. "A heck of a lot more than we do," she admitted. "It'll take some serious recon. We've got to be ready to explore and skirmish on land and sea, like you said at training last night. Let's put together a list of defensive supplies. And, don't forget, horses can't swim. We'll need to figure out how to handle them . . . and how to craft a boat that'll hold all of us—in case we need to move the mounts offshore to an island." She mulled over that possibility. "We're gonna need lots of food and potions, for sure. If we have to wait out the griefers, we might have to bivouac for some time."

"That's a *lot* of prep," Rob said soberly. He turned to Jools. "Consult with Stormie over the inventory. We don't want to get out there, only to find we forgot our swim trunks." Rob rose to his feet. "And get moving. We'll ride out directly after our museum field trip."

Jools nodded. "Perhaps we'll come back with something to add to the collection."

Rob said uneasily, "I'll be happy if we just come back."

*

Jools and Stormie worked side by side in the stable yard getting ready for the next campaign, Jools busy at the brewing stand while Stormie focused at the enchantment table.

"Between the two of us, an ocean monument doesn't stand a chance," Jools declared, laying out some pufferfish and magma cream next to his base potions. "The gold is ours."

"I wouldn't make loot a top priority," Stormie warned. "We could get a boatload of prismarine and ores, but how're we gonna excavate and haul stuff around while we fight off the griefers?"

"Did you *see* me at drill last night? I'll fend them off with one hand and mine with the other."

Stormie smiled, then said, "Don't get too cocky. Our last meeting with Termite was a draw, remember?"

Termite had escaped. And she'd said she could divine his plans before he could carry them out. "True," Jools said. "Termite likely knows every offensive and defensive piece we've packed already, as well as when we'll be on our way."

Stormie placed the diamond armor she'd enchanted in the stack of finished garments. "We should probably operate on the notion that the griefers know everything we know . . . even the stuff we're not really sure about yet."

"But we'll find out what they're up to."

"Once Frida gets back," Stormie said decisively. "She's better at what-ifs than any of the rest of us."

Stormie completed the armor enchantment and moved on to the diamond weapons.

Jools was cooking up a batch of fire resistance elixir. He added the magma cream to his awkward potion. "I've not spent all that much time at sea. Remind me why we need to worry about fire?"

"Lava—in underwater caverns. Lightning on stormy seas. Oh, and pirates shooting at our boat with flaming arrows and TNT."

"Pirates?" Jools smirked. "I don't believe they exist. You've been watching too many Disney movies."

"Jools." Stormie set the Efficiency II pickaxe aside. "You know as well as I do that anything valuable in the Overworld is fair game for the taking by somebody."

"Oh, sure. I'm saying I don't believe in the 'argh, matey' type of pirates, with eye patches and nasty parrots."

"I wouldn't rule that out. We might find a modified macaw or two."

"Just not Son of Blackbeard, or the like. I've used the silly pirate-speak settings on my server before, but ditched them when the novelty wore off."

Stormie's expression was serious. "No, no. Pirates really do talk like that."

"*If* there are, indeed, real-life pirates. Not saying you're wrong," Jools added hastily. "You have been 'round the Overworld and crossed the oceans blue. We'll pack for a skirmish with scallywags, just in case."

Jools set his fire resistance potion aside and checked the spreadsheet for the next items. "Plenty of underwater breathing and fire resistance—still to brew: night vision, healing, and regeneration. Blimey, I'll be at this all day."

"You? I've only managed efficiency and sharpness enchantments so far."

"What else do we need?"

"Ugh. Aqua affinity, depth strider, respiration . . . something else. What does it say on that spreadsheet?"

He scrolled down the page. "Protection."

Stormie sighed. "Ain't even started on the horse armor yet. Maybe you can help me when you're done." She paused. "Say, Jools. Do you ever wish you could just rewind to the beginning? Seems like the more you know about this game, the more there is to fuss about."

He gazed off toward the pasture. "Life as a newbie was sweet, true. Well, once I got rid of my so-called mates in multiplayer, anyway." He picked up an empty water bottle and turned it over in his hands. "What I'm finding, though, is that the more XP I get, the more I appreciate the nuances of this life. It's not just about lopping the heads off of zombies anymore."

She eyed him. "Ever think of going Creative?"

He set the bottle on the brewing stand. "I can't deny that I have. Build stuff all day, get lots of *ooohs* and *ahs* for your trouble. . . . Never have to watch for mobs. . . . There's only one thing that prevents me from doing so."

"What's that?"

He grinned. "Fear of boredom."

She smiled. "Copy that."

*A woman after my own heart.* Jools turned back to his work with a sigh. Stormie was a fearsome warrior, an artillery specialist, and a diehard globe trotter. He was just a detail consultant. She was way out of his league.

*

Turner and Frida came riding in the next morning on Duff and Ocelot while Jools was off spending some quality time with Beckett. Jools saw them come in from the west as he hand-grazed the palomino in a grassy thicket a little ways from camp.

"Oh, joy. The blowhard returneth," he said to himself. "Not sure I'm up to Turner's whingeing just now. At least he located Frida. I can use her help."

Frida: there was another of Battalion Zero's female troopers who was off-limits to the quartermaster's nonexistent advances. Jools knew the captain had a thing for her, but had never made a move. She was available. "Not that she'd ever in a million years consider a man like me," he mused. Among Frida, Stormie, and Kim, Frida was probably the toughest fighter. He knew she'd often faced survival challenges with zero protection and stayed alive based on her own wits. Whereas Jools needed every potion and enchantment he could get his hands on to keep hearts in his health bar. *No cheats, though; Colonel M was right about that. Some of us play by a code.*

In any case, he was not Frida's type—nor Stormie's, although she was kind enough to put up with him. Kim held some attraction, but Jools doubted a relationship with her would last long, given that she was so sweet and focused on the horses, and that he was . . . let's face it, a rather bitter geek. "But a proud bitter geek," Jools reminded himself, patting the grazing Beckett's shoulder. "Perhaps I'll meet a nice, dorky librarian someday and settle down. Have a bunch of html-code-writing tykes to care for us in our old age." Beckett raised his head from the grass for a moment. "Well, a lad can dream, can't he?" Jools asked. The horse returned to his grazing.

With the absent troopers back in camp, Captain Rob would want to pay a quick visit to the city and get packed up for the trail. "Best put on my quartermaster's bonnet," Jools said. He pulled Beckett's head away from his snack and led him toward camp.

In the interest of speed, the reunion with Frida took place on the short walk from camp to the Beta city gate. When the wiry vanguard spied Jools, she left Turner's side and ran up to sock him hello on the arm. He rubbed the spot and asked how her reunion with the clan had been.

"Fruitful," she said, tossing him an apple she'd brought back from the jungle oaks. An outline of the fruit pierced by an arrow was etched in ink on her neck, a symbol of her family solidarity. Frida came from a long line of jungle survivalists. Her olive-green skin and camouflage clothing seemed to have sprung from the biome itself.

Jools took a bite of the apple, chewed, and swallowed. "Ready to ride right back out again toward imminent danger?" he asked conversationally.

"Always," she said. "But first, let's get a look at the latest addition to the capitol complex. I hear the UBO museum is amazing."

"Bound to be a magnet for tourists. That's the plan, anyway."

"Anything to keep folks moving across biome boundaries," she said. "The only acceptable Overworld—"

"—is free and unencumbered. I know. We'll certainly appreciate your skills on this next foray to keep it so. But first: let's gobble some eye candy."

The troopers reached the new iron gate, to which twin iron golems were leashed. The city now had a

permanent stone wall where the chainmail construction fence had been only a few weeks before. An infan-
try unit trained nearby, with Burk barking out orders
as the recruits drilled.

"Danged newbie's wasting hearts on marchin',"
Turner grumbled.

Three small children mimicked the soldiers, stomp-
ing their feet in time and carrying twigs as swords.
Residents pushed carts of produce and mining supplies past the marchers, calling out to those they
knew. A woman stood on an upturned block address-
ing a small crowd regarding volunteer opportunities.
Beyond them, a steady stream of people moved in and
out of the new shops and public halls. Jools noted that
what had once been a building site populated only by
workers was now a bustling community. The citizens
of Beta owed much of their prosperity to Battalion
Zero.

Seeing the new improvements, Frida said, "What a
difference a month makes!" She hailed the builder, his
sister, and Judge Tome, who were approaching them.
"De Vries! Crash! You've been busy. Judge Tome. Nice
to see you."

The tall, lanky architect waved, and his short,
stocky sister notched some cobblestone from the
ground with her pickaxe in greeting. Jools noticed
a trail of chunked-up blocks lying across the capitol

compound, presumably mapping Crash's journey. The enthusiastic miner's imprint on the city was unmistakable.

The stately judge, dressed in his formal cloak, held out a manicured hand for Frida to shake. "Welcome home, dear," he said affectionately. The latest threat to biome unification had brought everyone closer together. Except, perhaps, the sergeant at arms and the newly minted lieutenant.

Jools trailed Turner as the mercenary stomped up the polished granite steps to the museum's grand entrance. The wide staircase led to a pillared vestibule, ringed with gemstone inlay.

"Looks way too much like a courthouse," Turner groused.

De Vries heard him, and in his lilting voice explained, "It's meant to echo the structure of the courthouse, yet stand on its own merits. Notice the artful detail here—"

Turner cut him off. "Let's get this over with, pal. Nothin' pushes my snooze alarm button quicker'n arts an' crafts."

Jools caught up with Turner, prepared to escort him through the galleries so he wouldn't touch anything. Perhaps he could help elevate the coarse player's sensibilities by acting as a helpful docent. *Or, at least, embarrass the heck out of him by displaying my vast knowledge of natural history and Overworld sculpture.* But Jools's ulterior motives were soon lost in the splendor that surrounded them.

The first hall held iconic relics from the game's past versions. Antique skins and obsolete horse saddles drew Kim's attention.

"Look! A pink skin!" she exclaimed. "Not as nice as mine, but still. Players were wearing them way back when. Hey, De Vries, did you know that these old horse saddles were mob-specific?"

"Yes. They couldn't be used on pigs," the builder confirmed, delighted at her interest. "We'll be putting fun facts like that one on little placards by each exhibit."

"Thrill a minute," muttered Turner.

Stormie pointed to a display case of once-fashionable clothing. "Look at these personal capes, y'all. Jools, weren't these capes doled out to the original language translators? Maybe there's one with a skull and crossbones on it for the pirate-speak interpreter."

They weren't able to find that, but some old transportation artifacts caught Jools's eye. "A vanilla minecart booster from way back . . . I'd put it at test release one-point-four," he guessed. "And look at these old skis! These have got to be Pre-Beta. There must've been a glitch that couldn't be solved. You can't even craft these anymore."

Jools continued his informative monologue as the visitors perused a group of mob and player statues. Judge Tome asked him a number of questions about early UBO art commissions, while Turner yawned and pouted.

Next, they moved into the Hall of Prehistory to find ancient fossils and evidence of tribal life now gone from the Overworld. This got Rob excited. "Look, guys! A petrified dragon egg!"

"Right next to arthropod fossils," Frida pointed out. "Ugh!"

"Silverfish are considered one of the oldest forms of Overworld life," Jools related. "They were erroneously thought to have come from the sea, hence their name."

"I don't want to know," she said, shuddering at the thought of her least favorite hostile creatures.

"Whoa! Shrunken mob heads!" Rob called from another case. He read the cards that identified them: "'Wither skeleton,' 'creeper,' 'zombie' . . ."

"Check this out," Kim interrupted from the other side of the aisle. "'Mummified skeleton.' Is that even possible?"

All of this natural and cultural history was lost on Turner, who hadn't said much at all. But as they entered the Hall of Armor, his eyes lit up like lottery ticket machines.

"Now, this is my kind of wardrobe," he said, nodding at a full suit of studded armor. "Think these was used before enchantments caught on. Looka that. Little studded boots, righteous-lookin' leggings . . . Here's a chest plate that'd make Swiss cheese out of a slime block. . . . If I got ahold of this stuff, I'd be the last man standing, for sure."

Jools burst the sergeant's bubble. "They're prototypes, Meat. Not functional."

De Vries added, "Circa Indev zero-point-three-one. For some reason or another, they were never implemented."

"Shame," Turner murmured.

The gallery held the most complete collection the group had seen yet. There were antique broadswords, stringless bows, chiseled stone tools, and finely fletched arrows. These were outdone by case after case of one-of-a-kind weapons from documented battles of the First War.

"The infamous diamond and obsidian sword-axe!" Frida whispered reverently.

"And here's the very first TNT cannon ever crafted," Stormie said, echoing her awe.

"Yes, something for everyone in this hall," De Vries said with pride.

Crash made her way to the head of the group and pointed her diamond pickaxe at the sign for the next gallery: HALL OF GEMS AND ROCKS. This was the only attraction that would have pulled Turner away from the display of arrowheads and fletching.

They took in the various specimens of common and unusual rocks. Jools pointed out that the diverse blocks demonstrated the Overworld's geological variety, from cobblestone to obsidian to prismarine. But the array of gemstones was truly mind-boggling: diamonds, emeralds, lapis lazulis of every size and cut—some rough, some polished, all stunning.

As they reached the far end of the gallery, Crash got their attention. She waved her diamond pickaxe and then set it in the middle of her forehead, like a unicorn's horn. She motioned for her brother to explain further.

"This, my friends, is what really takes the biscuit," De Vries said. "I give you the rarest gemstones ever unearthed—in any version of the game. Only five of these were ever found." After a suspense-building pause, he took a step back and swept an arm at the nearest glass case. "Ladies and gentlemen: our red diamonds."

Jools felt a wave of awe roll through the tour group. The stones were enormous—the largest gems he'd ever laid eyes on. Their hue was a deeper and clearer red than anything else in nature—almost liquid in quality, as though someone had poured pure color into them. Each one had been cut to perfection: four shining, sparkling, flowers of red, exhumed from the earth and brought to life in the light.

All at once, however, the viewers noticed the same thing: one of the red diamonds was missing.

# CHAPTER 6

"HOLY MOTHER OF ENDER PEARL!" TURNER exclaimed. "Got us a jewel thief on our hands."

"Why steal just one of the stones? And how?" A shaken De Vries got down on hands and knees to examine the bottom of the glass case. There were no signs of forced entry. He got up and explained to the group, "These valuables are secured via redstone circuit and weighted plates. Anyone removing one of them would have been instantly perforated by those." He waved a hand at the ceiling, where a cluster of metal spikes would be released if someone tripped the trap.

Crash threw down her pickaxe, motioned to the remaining stones, and then spread her hands to suggest a very large item.

"They ran off with the biggest diamond?" Jools guessed. "Of course."

"But why just one?" Kim asked.

"They knew it would hurt us more," Frida replied. "Think about it. If you have a set of matching pink armor and someone takes your helmet, even a gold replacement is gonna stick out like a sore thumb."

Kim considered this. "You're right. I'd rather have no armor than a lame set like that."

"Plausible explanation for swiping a single stone," Rob said. "But what about the bigger *why?*"

Jools had stepped up to repeat De Vries's inspection. "Likely, the object of a ransom demand," he said from underneath the cabinet. "It's not as if they're going to hock it on eBay." He crawled out and asked De Vries for a ladder. When the builder produced one, Jools placed it under the spikes and climbed up to examine them. Gingerly, he poked his fingers at the trap.

He gasped. "These projectiles aren't going anywhere." He descended the ladder and faced his friends. "Let me ask you this: have you ever tried to wash dried slime out of your laundry? The stuff is beastly sticky. I know. My tweed will never be the same after the last drill." He indicated the patch of foul residue on his sleeve. Jools turned to De Vries. "Your protective spike trap has been immobilized by the slime." He glanced from the spears to the case of diamonds. "Once that glorified snot hardened, it would've been a simple matter to disrupt the redstone circuit, remove the gemstone, and reroute the wire. Looks like it'd never been touched," he said admiringly.

"I'll find whoever did this," Turner growled, "they'll wish *they'd* never been touched." He opened and closed a fist.

"You'd like that diamond for your personal collection, eh?" Rob accused the mercenary.

"Not hardly." Turner said, offended. "Got a job to do, and I do it."

". . . or somebody else will take your place, *Sergeant,*" Jools pointed out. "Competition is a keen motivator."

"So is greed," Stormie said, putting her hands on her hips and shaking her head at the empty pedestal in the diamond exhibit. "Reckon we got our work cut out for us now, Captain."

"No doubt the two prongs of our mission are related," Jools said. "Although diamonds are not part of Termite's standard diet."

Now Frida leaned forward to examine the display case. "Sophisticated knowledge of redstone circuitry . . . brazen theft . . . This could point to another of Lady Craven's griefers: Volt."

Murmurs went through the group.

Jools mulled over Frida's thinking. An informant of theirs in the flower forest had recently been shaken down for a sizable number of emeralds and squash.

When pressed, she had dropped Volt's name. *Volt . . . possibly a redstone expert.* The redstone bomb that had threatened the battalion members might have been the work of an electrical engineer—not the crazed sociopath, Termite. Her army of silverfish had demolished Beta's wooden apartment structures and gold ore veins. *Cellulose and gold . . . typical arthropod fodder.* This Volt, though—he, she, or it—could have taken the red diamond for Lady Craven, to ransom to bolster the GIA treasury. Or Volt might have been the one who conceived the plot himself and sold the diamond to her. If so, the redstone expert would be long gone and might never be traced.

Jools joined Frida at the display case. The remaining four faceted jewels seemed to dance in the shafts of torchlight. "Have you ever seen a redder red?" Frida said quietly.

Jools allowed he had not. "Their singular beauty will make it easy to spot a fake." The puzzling theft represented the most baffling mystery the strategist had ever tried to unravel. To himself, Jools said, "I will find that stone, and the person who took it . . . if it's the last thing I do."

\*

Battalion Zero needed no further incentive to begin a search for allied or rogue griefer suspects. As they filed back through the city gates, Turner asked Rob, "You sure it's safe leavin' that toddler in charge o' security?" He jerked his head at Sergeant Burk, who was now running his troops through a series of calisthenics. "He's gonna work 'em to death before the zombies can."

Rob eyed the earnest settlers performing jumping jacks for their even more earnest commander. "They're young. They can handle it," the captain said, inferring that Turner wasn't and couldn't. "Besides, I put De Vries and Crash back on night duty." The brother and sister's alternate wolf skins made them effective undercover guards.

"I'll bet poor De Vries wishes they'd been prowling about last evening," Jools put in. "Rotten luck, that. It was perfectly rational to believe the security system would suffice. Crash indicated that she'd been in the mines and her brother had been working up plans for the city rail station all night."

Frida stopped on the path and looked back at the city. "I'm guessing the crook escaped by rooftop and over the wall. I couldn't find any footprints on the ground. Folks don't usually look up—I can see why nobody spotted the thief."

The troopers returned to camp, each of them readying either horses, tack, or supplies for the trip east. At last, they assembled at the minecart roundhouse. The six Thunder Boys scurried about, inspecting track and polishing already gleaming minecart siding. They chattered to each other in a language that Jools had never been able to grasp. He was pleased to see that a train of four carts stood waiting—one for passengers, one for horses, and two for freight.

Jools called one of the Steves over to help him load a chest of splash potions onto the freight car. The leather-clad rail worker noticed the picture of a shattered bottle next to the fragile label and wouldn't touch it. He unleashed a feverish diatribe, which the quartermaster assumed meant the lad didn't want to suffer the effects from an alphabet soup of broken splash potions. "Come on," Jools encouraged him. "Doesn't matter how you stack it. They're packed in wool, and Stormie's given all the crates fall protection."

Their language barrier prevented Jools's explanation from getting through to the young man. His mirrored sunglasses prevented Jools from knowing whether he'd been understood or not.

They stood there looking at each other for a moment. Then Steve pointed at a stack of wool meant for crafting beds. "Well, I suppose it can't hurt," Jools said, and the rail worker lined the freight car with wool. He called over two more Steves, and together they gently transferred the cargo to the cushion.

One of the other Steves was helping Kim load the horses, which she'd dressed in armor to save inventory space. The cavalry mounts had never seen the inside of a trailer before. The car had wood plank sides with spaces between the panels for ventilation and a roof for protection from sun and intruders. With the back door open, the car was essentially a dim box.

While Armor, Beckett, and Nightwind stepped warily inside and agreed to be leashed, Saber, Ocelot, and Duff would have nothing to do with the scary box—even with their friends inside. Duff stubbornly planted his feet and refused to move. Ocelot backed away across the tracks. Saber stretched out his neck toward the cart, snorted, and looked at Kim as though waiting for an explanation.

"We'll have to convince Saber first," she said. "Then the others will go in."

The nearest Steve started haranguing the stallion in another language, using hand gestures to emphasize whatever it was he was saying. This upset Saber, who began pawing at the ground but would not step up into the train car.

"Not like that, Steve," Kim scolded. "Talking means nothing to a horse. Body language is everything. And waving your arms is saying, *Look out! Don't go in there.*" She took the stallion's lead rope from the Thunder Boy. "Like this." She shut her mouth and, without looking at Saber, led him back toward the cart door.

He stopped.

She clucked and stepped up into the trailer cart, her back to Saber.

He looked at her, and then hesitantly put a foot up on the step.

She patted him and clucked again.

Saber thought this over, then put his other forefoot on the block.

She patted him again, moved into the car, and waited.

Saber gathered himself and leapt in, forcing Kim to scramble out of the way. Then the horse wheeled, stuck his nose back out the door, and gave an insistent whinny at his counterparts who remained outside, as if to say, *The coast is clear.*

Ocelot and Duff led Steve, who was holding them, into the cart. Kim leashed them and said to the mine-cart driver, "Less talk. More action. That's what horses understand."

Meanwhile, Turner and Stormie pushed several chests of weapons trackside, and Jools watched the Steves load them. Then Stormie brought over her single-block TNT cannon—her baby. "Easy, fellas. Careful, now. Let 'er down slow. . . ."

Jools felt a sudden surge of anxiety. Any operation that required artillery increased the probability of player death, obviously. He felt the weight of his convictions like never before. At least when he had remained steadfastly independent, he hadn't worried about whether he'd chosen the winning or losing side.

Kim must have read his thoughts. With her usual enthusiasm, she gave a rallying cry: "Come on, Bat Zero. Let's ride this train up to Lady Craven's doorstep!"

The horses and cargo loaded, the cavalry members marched into the passenger car. One Steve took the conductor post and one faded back to the caboose. Judge Tome had walked down from Beta to see them off. Jools saw his gold UBO ring flash in the sunlight as he waved. Then one of the Steves pushed the go button, and the minecart train pulled away.

Jools had checked in with Gaia to make sure the tracks that led to the ocean were still in place. The rail spur had materialized outside of Spike City one night without explanation. The priest had learned that the line led eastward and dead-ended at the ocean shore. She told Jools it was still there, and that tales of griefers and enchanted mobs continued to build around the area. He felt sure they were headed in the right direction . . . or in the wrong one, for a certain selfish player who wanted to avoid a fight. It was hard for Jools to shake off his old restraint. But, he reminded himself, the battalion was together, and—unlike the mates who had lured him into the game and dumped him—they'd have his back.

One of the Steves activated a train whistle sound effect, which galvanized the troopers onboard.

"Woo-hoo!" someone cried.

Turner shot off a fire charge.

Jools leaned out the window into the breeze as the train picked up speed. *Watch out, Lady C.,* he thought. *Ready or not, here we come.*

*

The trainload of cavalry mates and mounts journeyed southward over the steep, dry extreme hills and onto the frigid ice plains. They made good time. The sun was just sinking into the twinkling snow on the horizon as they passed Spike City and followed the rail spur to the east. Torches placed on the cart would allow the driver to see the tracks ahead, but wouldn't emit enough light to discourage the mobs.

Turner pulled some bows and arrows from his inventory and moved down the aisle handing them out to the troopers. "To skellies, this here train'll be an irresistible snack bar."

"A moveable feast, as it were," Jools agreed. "I'll take some of those party toothpicks, Meat." Turner gave him a stack of arrows and one of the short, reinforced bows he had modified for horseback combat.

They would be easy to maneuver through the windows of the passenger car.

Kim accepted her weapon and ammunition and said, "I'm going to go cover the horses. Anybody want to come with?"

"I will," Jools said.

Rob stepped in. "Two of us go up front and two aft, to cover the Steves." He motioned Turner and Frida ahead and Stormie with him to the caboose. They picked up their weapons and took their posts. Kim and Jools crouched on the tiny platform between the horse trailer and the passenger car, the darkened, snowy ground flashing by beneath them.

It wasn't long before the nightly zombie chorus began. *"Uuuuhh . . . ooohhh . . ."* The syncopated beat of bone clacking grew, its tone changing from snare to bass drum as the skeleton mobs closed in on the train. Jools realized they hadn't included this scenario in their training—shooting at moving mobs from a moving minecart. *Shouldn't be so much different from horseback. Then again, you never know.*

To Jools's pleasure, the first zombies to locate them were unable to keep up with Steve's preprogrammed speed. The few that managed to get handholds on the passing train lost them immediately—along with their hands or arms. *That'll teach them to try to stow away,* Jools thought.

Then some quicker baby zombies tried to hurl themselves through the open windows of the passenger car.

"Phew!" cried Frida, waving away the stench. "Somebody needs its diaper changed."

Turner wrestled with one tenacious tyke that had made its way inside. It grabbed his sword in its mouth and began sucking on it.

"You want a pacifier?" Turner yelled. "Go to *sleep!*" He pulled a diamond axe from one of his twin shoulder holsters and whacked the baby zombie's head off.

Still, more of them kept coming, launching at the open windows like undead human cannonballs.

"Turner!" Frida called. "Block 'em. Like this!" She raised a wood block that she'd been sitting on to window height and shunted the rotting infant back out into the night.

"An ounce of prevention is worth a pound of cure," Jools murmured, enjoying the entertainment.

Now baby cries joined the moans. The zombies gave up the chase, and the minecart train sped away. The sudden silence, but for the modified sound of chugging and wheels on rails, made the ride seem like a sightseeing tour.

Jools caught Kim's eye and joked, "Tickets! Tickets, please. All aboard the *Eastern Express!*" She giggled. "On your left, you'll see a bunch of whipped zombies shuffling off toward Spike City. The ice plains village, home of the fabulous Thunder Boys, is known for its modern ice spike condominiums. . . . To your right, you can see the stunningly beautiful frozen river, which forms the biome border to cold beach. Make your reservations for summer camping now—" He broke off. "What the devil?"

"Troops! Behind us! To arms!" Rob shouted.

Jools whirled around to see a wave of skeletons on horseback—and one on a chicken—storm up to the train from the rear. Their mounts were flesh and blood. The poor enslaved horses and bird ran alongside the cars while their jockeys fitted bent arrows to flimsy bows.

"Use your long-range weapons!" Frida cried from her post.

Kim stood up. "But don't shoot the horses!"

A shower of mob arrows hit the sides of the mine-carts, some sticking, some deflecting harmlessly. Only a few sailed through passenger windows or between the slats in the other carts.

The troopers opened fire, sighting to target the undead and not their mounts. Jools heard an equine grunt. An enemy arrow had hit Nightwind, dealing him minor damage. Kim saw red. She began firing arrows two at a time. "Die! Die! Die!" she screamed at the attackers. Two, then four, then six skeleton riders fell to the ground, disintegrating.

A jockey on a particularly swift steed managed to reach the first car. Jools saw it leap from the saddle to the roof of the passenger car and hug it.

"Mind the window, Meat!" he yelled to alert the sergeant to the intruder.

The skeleton kicked its leg bones over the side and dropped in through the opening. Turner had traded his bow for both diamond axes and was waiting. He snarled, "Double yer pleasure!" With twin blows, he separated the pile of bones at the waist. The top part fell to the floor intact. For an instant, both halves stood upright; then they toppled in a deafening drum roll.

"Five points!" Frida called.

Jools felt Kim gouge him with her elbow. She pointed. "That bunch went around to the other side!" The skelemob had split up and was trying to surround them.

Kim fired to the left, while Jools aimed to the right, picking off skeletons handily and leaving the galloping horses riderless. The chicken jockey was left far behind. After another stretch of skirmishing, the battle ended, and the train drew away.

"Too bad we can't stop and collect some of that herd," Kim said, looking wistfully after the retreating horses—and one chicken.

"Let's hope they find their way down to the taiga, where there's forage," Jools said, trying to encourage her. *She wants to save them all,* he knew. *I just want to save me and mine.* He wiped the sweat off his forehead and pushed through the trailer door to check on Beckett and make sure he was okay.

"Nice work, people!" He heard Rob compliment the battalion from two cars back.

The next moment, the ear-splitting sound of iron meeting wood filled the air. Jools slammed into Beckett's side.

Someone screamed.

Duff and Saber went down on their knees, and Jools saw Kim sail over them as the trailer car listed to the left. It tumbled over and over again, its contents with it, until the airborne minecart came to rest with a definitive *CRASH*.

# CHAPTER 7

*INECART TRAIN PLUS STATIONARY OBJECT. Result: derailment. Consequences? Damage, dismemberment . . . death.*

Jools stirred, surprised to find himself able to move. It took a few more moments to catch his breath and find his voice. "Kim! Battalion! Can anybody hear me?"

He jumped at the answering moans, but determined that their sources were human and animal, not undead. The creatures that limped out of the wreckage, though, staggered like the undead. The horse trailer car had broken open on impact with the icy ground. A light snow was falling. In the moonlight that shined through the snowflakes, Jools could see pairs of moving forms. These merged into four- and two-legged beings as his double vision waned.

*Probability of damage, from greatest to least: 1) Min-ecart train; 2) Players; 3) Horses; 4) Supplies . . . 5) Ego. How could I not have foreseen sabotage?*

Stormie had enchanted much of the cargo and all of the horse armor with Protection or Feather Falling IV. *Why didn't we just enchant ourselves?* The troopers and Steves hadn't been wearing armor; the iron min-ecarts shouldn't have needed any reinforcement. But, then, the tracks shouldn't have been barricaded.

Jools heard Rob and Stormie helping Steve from the caboose rubble. Turner shouted at Frida, who answered from somewhere up front. That left . . . *Kim!*

Jools struggled to his hands and knees and floun-dered among the horses. The shaken beasts were trying to navigate the twisted metal and broken wood slats that littered the ice beneath their feet. They slipped on rolling glass bottles that were strewn everywhere. "Corporal Kim! Where are you? Are you all right?"

When she didn't answer, his panic rose. *Keep it together, keep it together*, he reminded himself. The minecart body could have crushed her. She could've been thrown onto rocks. A horse might've landed on her. . . .

Then Jools spied a small riding boot. It was empty. Pain shot through him as he climbed to his feet. He ignored it, turning this way and that, trying to find Kim in the cold, snowy gloom. Stormie crossed the minefield of damaged carts and milling horses to help him.

"I can't locate Kim!"

Wordlessly, the adventurer began heaving debris aside as Rob joined them. "Guys." He motioned toward the largest horse silhouette. Nightwind was shuffling his feet a few blocks away.

The three sprang for the stallion, who also appeared to be searching for his mistress. Jools's mind riffled systematically through the pile of bent rails and smashed planks, searching for the shape of the missing riding boot . . . and, suddenly, recognizing it.

The tiny boot still encased a tiny leg—which was, to Jools's great relief, attached to the rest of the pink-skinned tiny body. But Kim's face was bloody and her eyes were closed. Snowflakes fell on her cheeks before melting away.

Jools couldn't hear her breathing over his own ragged wheezing. He checked her health bar. *A single heart!* Not much, but it was everything. "There, there, bronc whisperer," Jools murmured, choking. "You're okay—aren't you?" He willed her to be.

Now Turner appeared. "Frida's up front tending to the driver. Anything I can do?" Concern bled through his gruffness.

"Need some light," Jools barked. He stiffened as Kim's health bar dropped half of its remaining heart. *Hang on . . . hang on!*

Stormie had sent an ambulatory Steve for the splash potions. Her creative use of Feather Falling had left them intact. The young minecart tender returned with an armload of unwieldy bottles, but he hesitated, disoriented in the darkness. His leather jumpsuit was torn, and his sunglasses had been lost. Fear filled his normally stoic face.

"Over here!" Jools called out to him as Turner produced some torches. "And hurry!" In the glow, Jools examined the bottles, searching for those that contained red liquid. He snatched them from Steve's arms and swiftly tossed them at his fallen comrade. Jools held his breath.

One by one, hearts popped into the injured girl's health bar. Frida ran up to them looking grim, just as Kim's eyelids twitched.

"I think she's coming back to us!" Jools announced, and began breathing again.

Rob had been standing by, frozen, dreading the loss of the tiny trooper and kindred spirit. The cowboy and the horse master had become a team the day they'd met, when he'd tamed Saber. If it hadn't been for Kim and her herd, there would be no Battalion Zero. "I'll see to the horses," the captain said now, knowing it was what Kim would have wanted him to do.

"I'll help," offered Stormie.

Just then, Jools felt a searing heat in his shoulder and heard an unmistakable groan. *"Uuuuhh! Uuuuhh! Ooohhh!"* The zombies they'd shaken at the outskirts of Spike City had caught up with them, and the mobsters were not happy. Jools's gory assailant lapped at the blood that poured from the gash it had inflicted.

Jools nearly passed out from the smell and the pain. Before he could call for help, he heard the distinct sound of two diamond axes being pulled from two holsters. Turner growled, "Insult? Meet injury."

*Th-op! Thop!* The blood sucking stopped. For an instant, Jools saw only the hilts of Turner's deadly weapons sticking out the zombie's skull like rabbit ears.

"Might need a Band-Aid," Turner remarked.

The monster crumbled to bits, and Turner was pulling the axes up from the pile of rotting flesh on the ground.

White noise filled Jools's ears, and the darkness grew bright.

Then he fainted dead away.

\*

Jools awoke to see two beautiful, black eyes and two quite lovely brown eyes staring at him with concern. Kim and Beckett hovered over him.

"Wh-where am I?"

Beckett gave a low nicker under his breath.

"You're here," was all Kim could manage.

Jools half rose from the pile of wool he'd been lying on and glanced around. Someone had crafted an emergency shelter out of the wood blocks they'd brought along and lighted the place with torches. One of the Steves waved from a pallet nearby, his legs elevated on blocks. Jools took in the faces of his fellow troopers, scratched and bruised and fatigued. Six horses huddled behind a fence panel in one corner.

"We're all here. . . ." The scene flooded back, and embarrassment rose like a tide. *I conked out! But . . . I'd more than half a dozen hearts!*

Turner stepped forward. "You was white as a ghost," he said, for once, without mockery.

Frida approached the pair. "Your health seems stable, Lieutenant. We checked before we moved you."

"Yes, well. I believe I succumbed to mental, not physical, strain," Jools speculated.

This seemed to comfort Kim. "Your mind was in overdrive. You've been working awfully hard lately."

He felt a sudden warmth: *kittens, favorite sweater, hot water bottle.* He didn't think she'd noticed.

"I'd like to offer you a break, Quartermaster," Rob called from across the room. "But as soon as you're able, we need your help."

The warm glow increased: *singing tea kettle, roaring bonfire . . .* They cared. Even when he was up for Wimp of the Year Award, they needed him.

"Not a problem, Captain. I'll just—" He faltered, trying to rise.

Kim's small, pink hand pressed against his chest. "Take it easy, Jools. Just rest a minute. Captain? Why don't we bring him up to speed first."

Rob summarized what they'd learned during Jools's unplanned nap. The minecart tracks had, indeed, been sabotaged. Their train had hit oak and spruce timbers while driving full tilt. The first two cars had flown off the track and rolled. The freight cars in the rear had been shaken up, but remained on the rails when the couplings broke.

"And the horses?" Jools asked.

Kim took over. "They tell me Nightwind found me in a mound of wreckage. He suffered some from the skeleton attack and the zombies, but the armor enchantments kept him and the others from being damaged much in the fall. They only lost a heart or two—and we're hoping wheat rations will restore those. I'd like to hang onto our golden apples, if we can. Though I was prepared to break them out for you, Jools," she added, then paused. "You gave us a real scare."

He looked into her dark eyes. "So did you, Corporal." *Right moment . . . looking, listening . . . She's paying attention to you! Say her name, you prat!* "Corporal Kim . . ."

Her tender face was suddenly replaced by the captain's furrowed brow and shock of black hair as Rob took Kim's spot at the bedside. "Quartermaster! I need a consult ASAP. Are you ready?"

*Good question.* Jools looked over Rob's shoulder at the horse master. *Was he?*

\*

As the sun took over the moon's shift, Battalion Zero literally picked up the pieces. Jools—up and able again—calmed his own nerves with the comforting rhythm of managing the details of the crisis. Point by point, he helped Rob and the others sort through and address the fallout from the intentional accident. Not until they'd made repairs and restored health did anyone mention what was on everyone's mind.

"Who would do such a thing?" Stormie asked as they ate a small meal of bread and cooked pig. "Settin' a death trap for countless souls."

"Stranding people in this frozen wasteland," Jools added. "Bloody impossible to get a tan here, among other things." He was more of a sunflower plains type of guy.

Turner had a theory. "Screen o' trees sounds like the work of Precious and her gang."

"That rustler's *gang* had some turnover the last time we met," Frida reminded him of their timely deaths. "And I don't think Precious has got the connections to know about this mission."

"Who else would gain by taking us off the grid?" Stormie persisted. "That's the question."

"And it always has the same answer," Jools said. "Griefers, Incorporated." The troopers were silent for a moment. "I say we press on," he continued. "If anything's going to happen, it'll happen out there." He waved a hand at the horizon. From the flat expanse of the icy plain, the terrain resembled a frozen ocean, making Jools's words extra chilling. But the members of Battalion Zero had never let a little cold, or fear, or insurmountable danger throw them off track. "One for all, amigos," Rob said. "Let's see if we can't get this contraption moving again. If we hit cold beach today, we can make camp and use our beds to coordinate our spawn points there tonight."

Everyone but Frida nodded in agreement. She had no need to change her spawn point. Death simply wasn't in her game plan.

Rob added, "With one exception made for you, Vanguard."

Stormie offered to take over the caboose watch post for the injured Steve. Even after a healing potion and three pork chops, he remained splayed out on one of the passenger car benches. The Thunder Boy either didn't operate on the same health scale as the others, or he was faking it for the attention.

Before Stormie went on guard, the girls clustered around him, to the guys' dismay—but neither Turner nor Rob nor Jools would let on. Their talk turned deliberately to sports.

"How about those Dragons?"

"I know. Eighty yards for a touchdown!"

"I hear the Champs bowled a double-wicket maiden for a win. . . ."

The diversion didn't work. Jools couldn't understand their brand of football, and the only other person besides him who knew anything about cricket was Kim—and, now, she wasn't listening.

The tumultuous journey had taken its toll on the quartermaster. He finally stretched out on one of the other benches to rest until they reached their destination. He quickly fell into a deep sleep. The other troopers followed suit. When the train finally ran out of mine-cart track at the beach, Steve the driver had to blow his sound-effects whistle three times to rouse them.

The time-out renewed enough of the troopers' energy to allow them to build a safe place to spend the night. They dug, chopped, and stacked ice blocks into a four-lobed igloo—one part of the cloverleaf for bunks, one for horses, one for cargo, and one for everything else. Their last task was to move all the freight inside. Nobody considered the train secure any more.

Jools marveled at his cavalry mates' varied skills that, combined, allowed them to do so much more than they could have accomplished independently. Stormie and Kim had figured out how to craft patches for the smashed-up rail cars. Turner and Rob had cleared the blocked tracks. Steve, the driver, straightened out the bent rails. Jools tracked down every salvageable bit of their cargo and repacked it. And that was all on top of killing man-eating zombies and making bone necklaces of ex-skeletons.

Despite the obstacles, they had made it here to the water's edge. Cold beach spread in icy blocks to the north and south as far as the eye could see. To the east, the snow-covered sand met the frozen edge of the ocean. Who could tell where land ended and tide began? To the west was the spruce-lined border of the ice plains biome that they'd just left behind. The trees seemed to have accompanied them to the beach, and now were old friends that turned the battalion's crude ice shelter into a real camp. Frida sealed the travelers in with an ice block at nightfall. After all of the day's ups and downs, Jools felt curiously serene as he watched the horses enjoy their dinner in the stable section of the igloo. Kim walked over and crouched down next to him on the ice.

"Peaceful, isn't it?" she asked.

"For a change," Jools said wryly.

After a moment, Kim said, "It's funny. Now that the danger is over, all I can think about is looking forward to seeing new things. I stayed home on the horse farm so much before I joined the cavalry. . . . Now I can go places I've only seen in pictures."

"Sounds like you should tag along with Stormie more often." *No! No! She should tag along with* you. *And do what, Billy no-mates? Play computer games all day?* "If you want to see the world, that is."

"What about you?" Kim asked. "Don't you like to travel? You could come with us on a trail ride sometime."

For a brief spell, speech eluded Jools. *I've never taken an actual pleasure trip. . . . That would be novel. With two females . . . that would be even more novel. They'd likely only include me as their valet. Or as the horses' water boy. Or the geek who could crack the code to some jungle temple treasure chest. . . .*

When he didn't answer, Kim rose and backed away a step. "But it probably wouldn't be exciting enough for you . . . since you're used to intrigue and special ops, and stuff."

Jools cleared his throat and got to his feet. "Yes, well. You know what I always say: life is just one big Rubik's Cube, waiting to be solved." He looked at Kim's shining black eyes. *And you, bronc whisperer, are the most perplexing puzzle of all.*

# CHAPTER 8

THE NEXT MORNING, JOOLS WOKE TO THE SOUND of music and the smell of breakfast cooking. He was the last one up.

Before he recalled his latest coordinates, he thought he'd respawned in his past life, in cavalry camp. There, at the base of the extreme hills, the song of a troubadour and the aroma of mushroom stew had provided some small comforts to the weary troopers. Then his mental newsreel played its reality program: The griefer musician, Gratiano, had long since been exiled from Beta. Crop farming had replaced fungus mining. And Battalion Zero and friends were currently encamped at the very edge—not the very peak—of dry land.

The sensory overture continued as Jools joined his cavalry mates in the igloo's common area. "Something smells wonderful," he said.

"Kim's mushroom stew," Rob replied, slurping some from a bowl. "Frida scouted out a mushroom island this morning and brought us take-out."

*Did the survivalist never sleep?* Frida grinned from one end of the table, where she sat sharpening her sword. As Jools accepted his ration and a smile from Kim, he turned his attention to the recorded music providing the morning's soundtrack. It was coming from a miniature redstone jukebox that the two Thunder Boys had brought with them, judging from their possessive stance right next to the thing. Steve and Steve, dressed in their torn leather jumpsuits and minus their concealing eyewear, engaged in a frenetic dance that involved limb jittering and sudden leaps into the air.

"J-pop," Jools identified the popular musical genre that spoke to the lads' true origins. "The Empress, if I'm not mistaken," he pegged the singer. "A member of musical royalty not related to the Griefer Imperial Army in any capacity." He walked over to the jukebox and turned it down, and then took his place at the table someone had crafted while he was asleep. The two Steves slowed their gyrations and glared at him.

"Glad you could join us, Lieutenant," Stormie joked.

Turner threw a piece of bread at him. "Enjoy your beauty rest?"

Jools put a hand to his pale cheek. "How else do you think I maintain my fair complexion?" He dunked the bread into his mushroom stew and ate a bite.

"By hidin' under a rock," Turner said snidely.

*Ah. . . . Life is back to normal, I see.*

"Well, we'll all get plenty of fresh air and sunshine today," Kim said. "Tell him what's in store, Captain." Without waiting for his answer, she excitedly continued. "A sea voyage. A real adventure!"

Again, she surprised Jools—travel for travel's sake.

"Reconnaissance mission," the more practical Rob explained. "To locate a safe camp."

"That *is* an adventure," said Jools, cynically.

"To a mushroom island," Turner griped. "With next to no possibility of loot at the other end. What kinda adventure is that?"

Jools tried to distance himself from the mercenary's jaded viewpoint—even though he shared it. "Yes, but the probability of hostile mobs spawning there is extremely low."

"Ain't hardly a reason to leave dry land."

"Good griefer, man," Jools exclaimed. "Haven't you ever felt the lure of the sea? The call of the deep? The siren's song?" Turner stared at him as though he'd turned into a two-headed calf. "Why, when I was a lad," Jools continued, "I lived for our outings at Crane Beach. Innertubes, water wings, sand castles . . ."

"I thought you said you dreaded those holidays," Frida pointed out.

"I dreaded two weeks of proximity with my bickering family," he clarified. "For my part, I could hardly wait to dip my toe into the pond."

"That's good news, Quartermaster," Rob said. "Because, while you were sleeping, we unanimously chose you to helm our ship."

"Me?" Jools blinked at him. "Because I'm so well versed in the ways of Poseidon, a.k.a. Neptune? Or because I'm such a swarthy fellow?"

Turner opened his mouth to make a crack, but Rob cut him off. "Because you're the only one of us who has done it before."

Jools shot Stormie a frown. "I thought *you'd* dabbled in every biome environment in the Overworld, several times over."

"That's affirmative," she said. "But I've only been swimming in the oceans—not sailing."

*Hmmm.* Frida and Kim had been largely limited to the jungle and plains. Rob came from the high desert in his old world.

"What about you, Meat?" Jools goaded Turner, "You're saying you never went deep-sea fishing? A manly man like you?"

Turner looked uncomfortable. "I—er—don't much like deep water."

Jools had no experience actually operating a boat. He'd merely been cast away in one—lost, after his multiplayer pals had left him in the lurch one time. He couldn't admit that now, though, in front of Kim and the others. "Right, then," he said, pumping himself up for the challenge. "As long as we've a map and compass, let's hit the open seas."

"Navigation won't be a problem," Stormie informed him.

"Yeah," Frida said. "You can see the island from here. I swam out there in about ten minutes. We just need a boat to get the horses and stuff over there."

Jools deflated. "Oh."

*

The battalion members set a rendezvous date and said good-bye to the Steves as the minecart drivers prepared to return to Beta. The troopers and their mounts were bound for the nearest island in search of a secure site for a base camp.

They plundered the passenger minecart for the wood blocks and planks used as seating, to craft a large boat. Then, with all of their horses and inventory loaded, the cavalry soldiers became sailors for the ten-minute journey.

"This boat should have a name," Kim suggested just before they pushed off. "What'll we call her?"

Jools tried to think of something appropriate. The square, open craft projected all the personality of a kitchen cabinet. "Perhaps something related to the mission . . ." he said.

"Something like, *High Hopes*," Rob proposed.

Turner snorted. "Think positive, Newbie. More like, *Done Deal.*"

"Smashing!" Jools grabbed an empty glass bottle and cracked it over the boat's bow. "I christen thee, the *Done Deal.* May you live up to your moniker."

Beckett whinnied, and Saber echoed him. Turner and Stormie waded behind the boat and cast it off.

Kim's enthusiasm far outstripped the real nature of the trip. As they moved away from shore, she grasped the side of the boat with both hands and thrust her face into the spray kicked up by the boat's wake. "I wish we had that wave and tide mod," she remarked.

"I don't," Turner said shortly, holding onto one of the inventory chests for dear life. He called to Jools at the rudder buttons, "You sure you can keep this thing afloat?"

"Feels like I've been doing it all my life," Jools answered, thinking, *Good thing I'm an ace typist—and that this thing only has two keys.*

The day was pleasant, with faded-blue sky and ice-cube clouds above and a calm sea below. Looking back toward shore from the water, Jools could see freshets of melting frozen rivers spilling from the tree line to join the sea. The beach was deserted. They hadn't seen another soul since they arrived.

Jools leaned an arm over the side of the wooden boat. The water was definitely unfrozen and wet, but not as cold as he would have thought. It was a lovely shade of blue—not as violet as a lapis lazuli, nor green as an emerald. He matched the darker blue shadows on the water's surface to the cloud formations overhead. It made him want to fly.

Jools gunned the motor, but the *Done Deal's* slow, steady pace was already top speed. The cumbersome craft bobbed and dipped not due to swells, but to the shifting horses, chests, and human passengers. Still, he caught some of Kim's excitement at the change of pace and scenery. "Avast ye, Corporal," he called to her. "Can you bring this ship's captain a flask of something thirst-quenching?"

"Aye, aye, Captain!" she answered, reaching for some flower water.

"This doesn't constitute a promotion," Rob groused.

"You're in charge," Jools said. "I'll remember that when the swabs mutiny."

They'd been on the water for all of two minutes when Frida called, "Land, ho!" from the crow's nest—a box placed at the bow. The mushroom island lay a few hundred blocks off, to the north.

Turner's relief was visible. "Thought we'd never get there."

Then Frida sounded a second alert. "Battalion! Another ship approaching at four o'clock."

Jools glanced toward the open ocean. A boat was coming on fast. It must have been crafted with a special mod—it had several decks, two tall masts, and lots of sails and rigging. *Impressive.*

"Look!" Kim pointed. "A skeleton flag!"

The vessel flew a tattered black-and-white pennant that flapped in the breeze. It featured a skull and crossbones.

"You've got to be kidding," Jools mumbled.

"Pirates!" Stormie said, then she turned to Jools. "I told you so."

*

It was too late to mount a strong defense; Stormie's TNT cannon sat harmlessly in a storage crate for the short hop to the mushroom island. Nobody had anticipated trouble this early in the day.

"I'm sorry, Captain," Frida apologized to Rob. "I should've seen it coming. Too bad we didn't craft a telescope."

Stormie accepted the blame. "My fault. I should've included that in our supply list."

Their chatter was cut short by a cry from the approaching ship. "Ahoy, bilge rats!" came a guttural insult. "Make way for Black Lung Bob, scourge of the sea. Prepare to be boarded!"

The troopers reached for their weapons.

"And don't try anything: me guns're pointed right at yer belly."

Seeing a row of cannons aimed their way, they froze. Meanwhile, Jools frantically pushed buttons, trying to pick up speed, change direction, or do anything else that might transport the *Done Deal* out of range. Too late: the warship pulled alongside, and a plank was thrown between the two vessels.

A buccaneer in a weathered skin and a ratty officer's uniform strode across, his iron sword drawn. He knocked Frida off her block and announced, "Black Lung Bob is seizing this boat and all its cargo."

Kim gathered her courage and piped up, "What're you going to do with us?"

He pushed his black felt hat back on his mass of tangled hair and snarled, "Could be ye'll walk the plank . . ."

Jools was not impressed by this threat, so close to shore.

". . . could be Black Lung'll maroon the lot of ye on a lonely isle."

Again, the nearby island did not seem inescapable. *Termite would eat this tame rascal for breakfast,* he thought.

". . . could be Captain Bob'll let you all go. It's yer loot he's after," he concluded.

They relaxed.

"But maybe not! That's fer him ta know, and ye ta find out."

Now the troopers were more confused than anything else.

"And if we won't give up our loot?" Rob challenged the pirate.

Black Lung Bob held up a redstone trigger. Jools guessed it activated the cannons remotely. "Death!" The pirate appeared to reconsider. "Or fireworks," he said, eyeing the trigger mechanism dubiously. "One or the other."

Still, the uncertainty of the situation demanded compliance.

"Now, you'll pilot this barnacle bus to that lily pad, thar." He waved at the mushroom island. "Then, what's yers becomes Bob's." He laughed maniacally and returned to his ship, hauling in the gangplank after him.

Turner said under his breath, "I say we rush sailor boy when we get to land. It's six against one."

"What about his crew?" Stormie said.

"We don't know how many there are," Frida added.

With enemy guns trained on the battalion's boat, Jools could not disobey the pirate's command. He urged the craft forward until it nudged the island shore.

From the grassless plot of mycelium sprouted tree-sized mushrooms and a few real trees, which former inhabitants must have transplanted in dirt blocks from the mainland. The battalion's boat floated listlessly until Black Lung Bob ordered them all to disembark.

As Jools and the others stood holding their horses on the bank, their captor transferred the company inventory to his, commenting on the contents as he went along.

"Weapons an' armor—Bob's men will relish these. Hardtack and grub, splash potions . . . Ahoy! What's this?" He located the stash of gemstones they'd brought along for trading and crafting. "A king's booty!"

Finally, the pirate moved the chest that contained Stormie's TNT cannon. "Yar! What've we here? A child's toy?" He transferred it to his things. "This'll look right smart on Black Lung Bob's poop deck."

The defenseless battalion members stood idly on the beach.

"An' now, ol' Black Lung'll take his leave." He reboarded his ship and pulled in the plank.

"Aren't you forgetting something?" Rob said sarcastically. "What about our boat?"

Turner hissed, "Can it, Captain!"

But Black Lung Bob just laughed again. "That chum trolley is the sorriest craft on the seven seas. Keep it!"

And with that, he sailed away.

The defeated troopers milled about with the horses. Stormie, however, drew something flat from a satchel that had escaped the pirate's notice. She spread a parchment on the ground and knelt down to study it.

Jools noticed. "Artilleryman! Your map."

"Been working on it for some time now," she murmured. "Kim and I plotted out this whole coastline and everything we could see from shore." She stood up again and waved at the retreating ship as the others listened in. "Given his course, I'd say Bob's bound for the next mushroom island to bury his plunder. It's not but a thousand or so blocks to the north."

"Could we make it there in this thing?" Jools asked.

"Don't see why not."

Rob took command. "People! There's no time to lose. We can't give up all those valuables. Volunteers for a pursuit mission?"

Jools and Turner put up their hands at the same moment.

"He called my boat a chum trolley," Jools said indignantly. "A sea captain's got his pride to uphold."

"I'ma show that sailor boy a thing or two about plunderin'," Turner threatened, socking a fist into a palm.

"Let me go with you," Kim said fiercely. "If there's one thing I can't stand, it's a common thief."

"He's common, all right," Jools agreed. He looked at the angry mercenary and irate horse master. "And he doesn't know what he's up against."

# CHAPTER 9

STORMIE SUGGESTED DISGUISING THE BOAT WITH mushroom flesh so it would blend in with the next island. "Maybe Black Lung won't see y'all comin'."

"Brilliant," said Jools. "The element of surprise makes a satisfactory substitute for weaponry, in this dire case."

Stormie and Frida punched down some red-and-white mushrooms and hung their speckled flesh from the sides of the boat. On the open water, the *Done Deal* would stand out. Jools would need to sail directly to shore without being seen. Once there, the camouflaged boat would provide some cover. Kim convinced Jools and Turner to wait until dark to sail, to increase the odds of a successful sneak attack.

Jools ran the scenario in his mind, firming up a plan as he went along. *We "ninja" our boat up to shore near the pirate ship. First, get a head count on Bob's crew and gauge his firepower. Next, locate our inventory. Lastly, create a diversion and re-swipe our goods. Post-script: make a clean getaway.*

He shared this preliminary plan with the battalion.

"Sounds . . . sound," Rob pronounced.

"Sounds simple," Turner said, chomping at the bit to get started.

"Maybe too simple," Kim warned. "With no weapons at all? We're not used to that kind of situation." She gestured at the vanguard. "Frida? How would you handle it?"

Frida checked the sun's place in the sky. "We've still got some time before dusk. Let's explore the island and see what kinds of arms we can put together."

They quickly dug a pit corral to secure the horses, and then took a few moments to survey the landscape. The day, as Kim had forecast, was sunny and balmy, with a fresh breeze blowing in off the ocean. Scattered chunks of clouds drifted lazily overhead. The caps of the huge mushrooms and crowns of the few spruce trees that somebody had planted swayed gently in the wind. *If only we were on holiday,* Jools thought, *it'd be peachy.*

The cavalry mates marched along behind Frida, up and down the steep mycelium slopes. An unusual lowing sound drew their attention to a cluster of hybrid cows in the distance. Their spotted hides represented ready sources of leather, beef, milk—and mushrooms.

The mooshroom cattle, they'd expected; but they were all pleasantly surprised to find more varied resources than they'd thought possible on the island. Streams and ponds provided ample fresh water. Kim squealed upon finding a few patches of wheat that they could feed the horses. Four mature mooshrooms and a couple of calves were already grazing there. They were red and white, and sprouted darling little red-and-white mushrooms instead of horns and tails.

"Aw," Kim admired the little ones. "I thought foals were cute, but these mini mushroom cows are, like, enchanted with cuteness."

"Like a cross between baby cows and baby vegetables," Jools observed. "You'd think restaurants would go bonkers over them."

"Watch this," Turner said and rigged a bow with a flaming arrow. He sent it at one of the grown animals and set it on fire. It dropped some leather and three grilled steaks.

"Better to farm 'em and get milk and mushroom stew," Frida said.

"Lots to eat here," Rob said. "And supposed to be nearly zombie free? I'd consider this island for a base camp if we can defend it from griefer invasions."

"And pirates," Jools said drily.

Frida and Turner punched at a spruce tree for its wood, and fashioned crude pickaxes for the group. Then Frida led them toward a likely-looking hollow in a hillside to do some exploratory mining.

Rob soon hit stone. They used the dropped cobblestone to upgrade to stone pickaxes. Then the work went more swiftly.

"Hot ham 'n' eggs!" Turner exclaimed upon notching into an iron ore deposit flecked with redstone. "I hit the jackpot."

"Quick!" Jools said. "A furnace!" He chunked up some more stone and used the drops to craft a smelter.

In the brief window remaining before the sun dove behind the mainland for the night, the cavalry mates crafted iron swords. By the time Kim, Turner, and Jools's squadron set sail, they were considerably better prepared to mount an offensive against the griefer pirate. Their friends watched with guarded optimism as the volunteers shoved off into uncharted waters.

"Farewell, me hearties!" Jools called, sounding more sure than he actually felt. "We'll be back before you can say 'Black Lung Bob'!"

\*

The three troopers set a northward course. Kim stood at the helm near Jools, enjoying the scenery, while Turner crouched nervously in the middle of the boat. Around his middle, he wore a flotation device crafted from spongy mushroom tissue. Jools and Kim knew better than to mention the mercenary's need for a life preserver.

The detailed quartermaster glanced overhead, cataloging the distinct quality of light created by the reflection off the vast body of water. "I'd forgotten how lovely a sunset could be," he said, as Kim basked in the fading streaks of color.

But when night fell, pleasure took a backseat to the job ahead. Kim climbed up front on the crow's nest and squinted at the moonlit sea. Jools silently watched her. Every now and then, a ray of light would glint off her golden earring.

Before long, Kim spied the fuzzy, dark outline of Black Lung Bob's vessel. "The pirates are moored in a little cove," she informed Jools and Turner. "If we can slip past them, we could drop anchor between ship and shore."

"Aye, aye," Jools replied, identifying their target and following the route she pointed out. When they'd successfully slid past the sleeping pirate ship, he whispered, "Quiet, mates," and gestured for Turner to lower the anchor they'd fashioned from a block of stone and the horses' lead ropes. The *Done Deal* came to a halt. "One of us should swim out first and test the waters," Jools said softly.

Now that the boat sat in the shallows, Turner channeled his anxiety into aggression. "Let me at that glorified pickpocket," he growled under his breath.

"No. Let me do it, sir," Kim petitioned the skipper.

Jools nodded. "She should go," he said to Turner. "She's the smallest and most likely to get in without notice." He handed Kim a lump of redstone ore. "Once you've surveyed the deck and found an unguarded entry point, flash this at us three times. We'll join you in three shakes of a lamb's tail."

Without another word, she slipped over the side of the craft and silently swam off.

A cloud sailed in front of the moon, and Jools lost sight of Kim's small frame in the inky water. He fretted as the minutes passed. The corporal hadn't hesitated to undertake the dangerous errand, not knowing what lay ahead of her. But it shouldn't take her too long to climb aboard and count men and guns. *Where is she? I could've respawned fifty times by now!*

At last, Turner dug an elbow into his side when he saw three short bursts of light flicker and end abruptly. The two of them dropped into the bay and pushed their way toward the resting warship. Turner's bulky float and dog paddling made more noise than Jools would have liked.

As they approached the hull, they heard voices and saw the warm light of a sea lantern glowing in one of the fore portholes. They headed for the dim area in the ship's stern where Kim's signal light had come from. It was simple enough to shimmy up the anchor rope and onto the deck.

"Over here!" came Kim's furtive voice from behind a stack of crates. The clouds had parted, and Jools could see her tiny, pink hand wave in the moonlight.

Turner slung his life preserver over one shoulder, and the two men sidled over to Kim through the shadows.

"The gun ports are shut, sir," she reported. "I can't tell if the crew is armed or not."

"How many are there?" Jools asked.

"I couldn't get a look inside." She jutted her chin at the filthy porthole. "But from the sound of it, there're four or five. The captain's in there with them."

"And the inventory?" Turner whispered.

Kim pointed to a sign over a doorway: CARGO HOLD.

As they crept forward, a loud squawk pierced the air. All three troopers dropped to the deck. They heard more squawking and an insistent beating of wings.

"Yarr, Salty Pete! Leave off!" Jools recognized the pirate's muffled shout, coming from the lantern-lit berth. "Ye've cried wolf one too many times, you dirty bird."

One more half-hearted squawk trailed away, and a mangy chicken pecked its way across the deck and out of sight.

Kim, Jools, and Turner waited until all was quiet again. Then Kim led the lieutenant and sergeant to the cargo compartment and pushed at the stubborn door.

"Must be warped!" she whispered. Turner waved her aside and shoved his weight against it.

With a loud squeak, the plank door gave way. The three friends crept down a short staircase and into the damp hold. "Pee-ewe," Jools said under his breath. "Could use a shot of Febreze." He stumbled over a loop of spider-string rope. He could see nothing but shapes in the thin creases of moonlight that shined through the cracks in the walls and the soot-smudged portholes.

Kim withdrew the chunk of redstone and cupped it in her hand, letting out just enough light to see where they were going. They spread out to survey the locker.

"Over here!" Jools said, recognizing Kim's set of pink-dyed armor in an open chest. All of their property sat there in various heaps. "Looks like Black Lung Bob isn't much for housekeeping," Jools remarked. He motioned to his friends to start loading the items into their inventory slots.

"The TNT cannon's too big to carry!" Kim complained. She called to Turner. "Maybe we can float it back on your innertube."

He grunted. "I'ma need that innertube. Find somethin' else around here that floats."

"Better yet . . ." Jools said, squinting through one of the cloudy windows and spying a small boat. "There's a dinghy out there we can load the bigger stuff into."

Turner stopped what he was doing. "I see everything here except our gems."

"What do you think Bob did with them?" Kim asked.

Jools began poking through the hold again. "He's a pirate. He'd have put them in a treasure chest . . . like this one." He grabbed one end of a black chest emblazoned with a skull and crossbones, and shook it. "There's something in here!" he said excitedly. "I'll have to pick the lock." He tried a few command variations. The first four didn't work, but on the fifth try, he heard the lock give. The lid slowly opened on its own.

"Well, I'll be—" Jools leaned over the chest and reached in. "There's more than just our loot in here!" The amount of wealth beneath his fingers sent a surge of greed through him like he'd never felt before. Turner dropped the axes he'd been sorting through and made a beeline for the quartermaster as he started scooping gems and gold pieces into his inventory.

Then something in Jools's hand brought him up short. "I must be seeing things," he whispered.

"What is it?" Kim called.

Jools drew the item from the crate and stared at it.

*"What is it?"* Turner asked impatiently.

Jools clutched the item to his chest and glanced from one friend to the other. "It's the red diamond."

\*

*Loot, beauty, prestige . . . the man who possesses this jewel can have it all! This is the most valuable thing I've ever held in my hand. Riches, recognition . . . the world is mine!*

The look in Jools's eye showed his thoughts to be adrift, far out to sea. "Lieutenant?" Kim said uneasily. "Are you okay? You're scaring me."

A moment later, footsteps could be heard above them, moving rapidly toward the cargo hold. The next instant, a figure burst through the door and down the stairs. "Belay there!"

Jools looked up to see Black Lung Bob pointing a gold sword at him.

"Drop the bauble, an' back away, ye scurvy—"

"Gotcha!"

There was a short scuffle, and the gold sword traded places between the ship's captain and the sergeant of

Battalion Zero. Turner had managed to slip behind the griefer when he came in the door. Now he held his own iron sword plus the golden blade at Bob's throat.

"I'd watch how you throw that 'scurvy' tag around," Jools said calmly. "We're all as hale as oxen. We've been dining on mushroom stew, which is quite rich in vitamin C." He made a show of appropriating the red diamond and securing it in his personal stores.

"Yarr," the conquered captain said woefully.

Kim ran to Jools's side. "You've got it, Lieutenant! That's a great big part of our mission accomplished."

"Music to my ears," Jools murmured. "Let's get out of here before the others show up."

"Not so fast," Turner stopped him. "Got a few questions for the skipper, here, before we go." He motioned with his head for Kim to shut the open door. "Now, who're you workin' for?" Turner jabbed a sword hilt into the griefer's Adam's apple.

The man groaned but blurted out, "Black Lung Bob works for no man."

"How about a woman, then?" Kim pressed. "Is it Termite? Lady Craven?"

Turner dropped one sword and hooked an arm around Bob's throat. "The truth! Answer her!"

"Bob spins no yarns," his prisoner gargled stubbornly. Turner loosed his hold to let the griefer speak. "Bob might've taken from the rich, the better to get richer. . . ." He hesitated. "Or the fella who gave up the stone might've traded it for Bob's redstone comparator." He looked Turner in the eye. "Or it may be that Black Lung Bob just likes pretty things." He gave an ugly smile, revealing several missing teeth.

Turner swiped the gold sword across one of the pirate's cheekbones, drawing a bright stripe of blood. "How's that for pretty? I'll ask you again: who're you workin' for?"

The pirate paused, and then replied, "One man, an' one man only: Black Lung Bob. Bob took that gem from a dandy in a fancy boat. It'll fetch at least a few ender pearls on the black market."

"A few pearls?" Turner growled and threw the pirate to the ground. "Only thing I hate more'n a parasite is a cut-rate one. That there stone is priceless."

The pirate glared up at him. "Everything has a price."

Now Jools strode forward and uncoiled a length of spider-string rope. "Bully. Then your men will be glad to pay your ransom." Kim helped him tie up the struggling captain. Jools demanded, "Tell us: how many men on your crew?"

When he didn't answer, Kim prompted, "How many? Four . . . five? More?"

Turner kicked the downed man to get at the real story.

"None! None, I tell ye."

The three troopers exchanged glances.

"But—your guns and sails . . . You must need a crew," Kim said to the pirate. "I heard you all talking. In your berth."

Slowly, the griefer explained, "It were a recorded book. *Treasure Island.* Black Lung Bob was just getting to the good part," he said bitterly.

"Then, how—?"

"I believe I know," Jools interrupted her. "Redstone technology. This boat's on autopilot."

"Yarr . . ." The pirate gave him an admiring look. "Ye got me."

In no time, they had hustled Black Lung Bob above deck and lashed him to a mast. The cavalry mates loaded their inventory, plus some extra loot, into the waiting dinghy and lowered the boat on spider strings.

"Ye can't leave a man like this!" the pirate shouted. "Curses! Bob won't rest till the last of ye resides in Davey Jones's locker!"

They left him bellowing into the night and sailed the small, rickety vessel laden with chests back toward their moored boat. They lashed the two together, and Jools steered the coupled crafts back toward the other mushroom island.

"We did it!" Kim cheered. "Wait'll the battalion hears about this."

"My plan was somewhat stellar," Jools said modestly. "By this time tomorrow, I'll warrant we fill in the remaining holes in our mystery and put the entire GIA on notice. I can't wait to hand Termite her severance slip and tell her she's sacked."

Turner stood up unsteadily, rocking the boat. Kim and Jools followed his gaze across the water, off toward the east. "Hold onto your helmets, gang," he said ominously. "Another ship coming in fast at ten o'clock!"

# CHAPTER 10

**W**ITH THE MOON AT ITS HIGHEST POINT IN the sky, the oncoming vessel was clearly visible against the shining water. It was a silver powerboat shaped like a wingless fighter airplane, and it barely seemed to touch the waves it created in its wake. The modified vehicle might just as easily have been streaking across the sky or flat terrain. It flew no flag and showed no guns, to Jools's great relief.

The troopers drew their weapons anyway. Turner still held the pirate's gold sword. Kim and Jools retrieved their enchanted diamond blades from the company inventory that they'd reclaimed.

The brave display belied their disadvantage. The two vanilla boats could be swamped in an instant by a sideswipe from the larger motorized craft—and Turner wouldn't like that. Jools cut him a look and saw that the mercenary's usual ferocity had been dampened by his dread of deep water. *Oh, no. Now is not the time for your sensitive side to surface, Meat!*

They all hung onto the sides of the *Done Deal*, which bobbed crazily as the other craft drew near and idled its engine. They heard static, followed by a message transmitted from inside. "Let's make this simple, right? Your gems—my inventory—chop, chop. You know the drill." The speaker crackled again. With a hum, a long pole with a net on the end of it swung out from the hull and stretched toward the squadron's boat.

The three friends stood motionless. Jools broke out in a sweat. *Nooooooo! My beautiful crimson treasure. Must . . . not . . . lose . . . diamond! Must not lose* life. *Diamond or life? Life? Or diamond?*

Turner never waffled over this kind of trade-off. Without moving his lips, the sergeant stage-whispered, "Hey. Be ready for loud stuff."

There was no time for Jools to argue. In one motion, Turner slipped his life saver over his head and launched a rocket at their adversary.

The *BOOM!* was followed by a spray of red and green sparkles—harmless, really, but it sounded destructive. As Turner had hoped, the griefer overreacted to the explosion and gunned the motor, lurching the powerboat too hard to the left. It rolled several times on the water's surface, righting itself a dozen blocks away. Meanwhile, Jools got their crafts moving in the opposite direction.

Kim checked over her shoulder. "It didn't sink! It's turning this way again."

Turner swore under his breath. "I don't dare use TNT this close to . . . us. Ideas, Lieutenant?"

Jools had never had fewer ideas—positive ones, anyway.

The pursuer caught up with them. Again an amplified voice came over a speaker: "I know you've got the diamond. Ools, lad. Din't ya hear me the first time? The loot. *Now.*"

Kim and Turner stared at Jools. Jools, pale as snow, goggled at the windscreen of the powerboat and whoever sat behind the tinted glass.

"Why did he call you 'Ools'?" Kim whispered. He ignored her.

*Vocal range . . . people I know who call me that . . . strike that; people I* knew *. . . Narrowing, narrowing, one of two possible—* "Whitney?" *I'm sure of it.* "Have you forgot your manners? Oh, wait. You never had any." Now a surge of old anger, sorrow, and a vicious sense of propriety bubbled up inside the quartermaster. He'd been the object of too much theft lately.

Jools jumped to his feet and tightened his fists. "You want what's ours? You'll have to take it!" He wagged his head at his friends, murmuring, "Chap I used to know. Don't worry. He's all bluster."

The speaker crackled. "All right, then. Have it your way."

Another automatic arm, fitted with a wooden axe, reached out from the powerboat and tapped the dinghy. The fishnet swung out right behind it. As the cavalry mates watched in shock, the dinghy reacted to the attack by dropping itself, and its inventory. The TNT cannon and treasure chest were swiftly retrieved.

"Hey!" Jools called at the unseen pilot. "What about old times' sake?"

"Took that into account," said the voice. "I'm lettin' ya live, aren't I?"

A muffled laugh escaped from the sealed compartment, and the streamlined boat pulled away in a wide arc, heading out to sea.

The rollercoaster ride of finding the diamond, nearly losing it, and then definitely losing it had shaken Jools to his core. He felt a small hand on his shoulder and glanced up. Kim looked sympathetically into his eyes.

"I—don't know what to say," Jools mumbled. "We've got to chase after him! I never thought that twaddler would go through with it," he added darkly.

Then Jools realized that Turner hadn't attempted to kill him yet. He twisted around to find out why.

He gasped. "What the—? Kim? Where's Meat?"

She turned and saw that the back half of the boat was empty. Turner was gone.

\*

"Sergeant? Turner?" Kim ran from one side of the dinghy to the other, peering into the depths. "He must've fallen over!"

But they'd heard no splash . . . nor any swearing. Frantically, Jools returned his eyes to the silvery wake of the retreating powerboat . . . and the small "tail" it was trailing that hadn't been there before. Squinting, he made out a doughnut shape, with two sticks kicking out of it. "There! It's him. It's got to be!"

Kim followed his gaze. "He must've hitched a ride."

Jools should have been comforted, but all he could think was, *He'll get the stone! Then we'll never see him again.*

"I'm certain he'll be fine," Jools lied, taking Kim's hand reassuringly.

Neither of them knew whether to stay or go. So they did nothing.

As they waited—for what, they knew not—Kim said quietly, "You knew that person driving the boat. Was it . . . someone from your past? Your old world?"

"One of the fellows I told you about—the fair-weather friend who found loot more appealing than genuine human feeling of any kind."

"Was he one of the multiplayer gang that left you stranded at sea?"

"Ironically, no. He left me battling for my life on a cliff full of zombies. I chose to dive into a lava waterfall instead of skirmishing with a broken pickaxe. Death number one-fifty-four." He smiled without mirth. "Good old Whitney. Wait'll I catch up with him again."

"I hope I'm there with you," Kim said, resolutely.

This moved Jools. "As do I. You're—you're a good friend, Kim." The compliment pleased her, but his own brain was floored. *You said what, now? The right thing? The sincere thing?* And just as he worked his courage up, the tiny devil inside him argued, *Fat lot of good it'll do. Considering you're either about to die at sea or return to camp in disgrace. This might be a good time to desert.*

Kim said nothing, and they settled into silence. When the sky began to show purple around the edges and the sun peeked over the horizon, Jools knew it was time to go. He punched the boat's forward button. With a last look over his shoulder, he set sail for the mushroom island where they'd left their friends.

How would the battalion take this little setback? The trouble with doing good work consistently, Jools thought, was that one little mistake could ruin a lifetime of effort. He worried that Rob, Stormie, Frida—and Kim, too—would remember only his misstep.

Kim put that concern to rest when they reunited with Rob and company on the island's beach. "Captain! The lieutenant's plan went off without a hitch."

Rob appeared puzzled, considering that Turner was missing, along with their oversized and precious cargoes.

Frida looked at Stormie. "They did manage to ditch the pirate . . ."

"But, I don't see my cannon anywhere," Stormie said worriedly.

"Or the diamond," Frida added.

"We stole everything back from Bob," Kim insisted, "thanks to the lieutenant."

Jools blushed. Stormie brightened.

"It's true," he said. "We did recover all of our possessions. Before losing them again."

Stormie frowned.

Kim wouldn't back down. "The mission went just like Jools said it would—and then some. He found the red diamond in Black Lung Bob's treasure chest!"

This impressed the group.

Jools shook his head. "But we lost it a short time later." He felt the beautiful diamond's absence like a searing hole in his chest.

"There was nothing you could've done about that," Kim said.

Together, they detailed the series of fortunate and unfortunate events in their lost-and-found adventure.

"Now, let me get this straight," Stormie said, trying to find an upside of the affair. "Y'all snuck onto the pirate ship unseen. That's good. You got our stuff back, and you found the irreplaceable diamond, to boot. Even better. Then, along came an old pal of yours, Jools, who swiped the diamond, every stone in our gem stores . . . and my TNT cannon? That's bad."

"But you did wind up with our armor, weapons, potions, and such," Frida said. "Not to mention, the *Done Deal*. And this cute, little extra boat! That makes up for some of the bad."

"Except for my cannon." Stormie folded her arms.

"*And*, assuming Turner comes back," Rob put in, "he might at least know whose hands the diamond fell into."

"That's some important intel," Kim insisted.

"It could show us our next step," Rob agreed. "In the meantime, we'll keep working on the other half of our mission. While you three were gone, we scouted the island coastline a ways. I think we found a pattern."

This cheered Jools up. He'd learned that when trying to get to the bottom of things, noticing patterns allowed him to spot the deviation. That usually provided the answer he was looking for.

"So, the effort wasn't a total loss, I suppose. Unless you count Meat."

"Now, now. The jury's still out." Rob sighed. "Not to sound too offhand, but the sergeant generally does turn up, eventually . . . whether you want him to or not."

*

In the squadron's absence, the remaining troopers had built dirt and stone shelters, one for horses and one for people. They hadn't been visited by any mobs other than passive mooshrooms overnight. They'd shared worse situations, Jools recalled. Maybe they could salvage this mission, after all.

If nothing else, they had located a suitable base for training and further oceanic exploration—if they ever had another reason to leave dry land. Just as Kim and Stormie had experienced, the shore had grown overnight. Or the ocean had shrunk. It was as though, little by little, some unseen force was crafting a boardwalk out of sand and gravel blocks.

"Now, I do love the beach," Stormie said. "But not at the expense of the ocean."

"I still think you're seeing just the effect and not the cause," Jools responded, "but I can't quite get my head around it. Give me some time. I'll go have a look myself . . . after a bit of a lie-down. Didn't sleep a wink last night."

*Nancy Osa*

The adventure had been so trying that he and Kim both nodded off and slept until the next day. Sure enough, Frida counted some extra beach blocks on the island before they woke. After breakfast, they saddled up the horses to ride out for a firsthand examination. Duff called vehemently to his buddies from the pit corral as they left him behind.

There wasn't much to see. An extra sand block here, another gravel block there . . . and no evidence of anyone trespassing. It was the most featureless set of clues Jools had ever tried to categorize. The only pattern he could discern was that the problem seemed to repeat itself overnight. Somewhere in the back of his mind lay a solution . . . but it was as slippery as a wet squid.

"Turner might have some insights, when he gets back," Frida said. Jools thought, *Probability: ten percent.*

"Until then," Captain Rob said, "the best thing we can do is stay sharp." He glanced around the immediate area. The beach was wide enough now to run some drill patterns. "Pop quiz. Frida, team up with Stormie. Kim, you and Jools are sparring partners. Use your wooden blades." He reined Saber backward under a tree-sized mushroom, then set the ground rules: "Okay, let's have some mounted melees. Your choice. A tap equals a death blow. We don't want to waste any healing potions. Stormie and Frida first." He waved the partners to opposite ends of the open stretch of beach. "You get hit, you take the sidelines and wait for my word. And . . . begin!"

With a little grunt, Stormie launched her black-and-white horse, Armor, at little Ocelot. Although the pony's brown spots nearly jumped off her black rump in readiness, Frida's mare obeyed her rider and held her ground. "Take that!" yelled Stormie, swiping at Frida with her wooden sword as Armor galloped past.

Frida simply legged Ocelot into a turn in place, taking them inches out of range and conserving energy. Then, before Stormie and Armor had completed their charge, Frida sent Ocelot after them. A mycelium outcropping forced the first pair to slow and turn. Frida took the opportunity to slap Stormie's behind with her wooden sword.

"Yikes!" Stormie had to grin. "You win."

They pulled back to watch Kim and Jools spar.

"And, go!" cried Rob.

Jools drew his stick sword and nudged Beckett into a measured lope heading straight for Kim on Nightwind. Like Frida had done, Kim telegraphed readiness to her mount but made him wait. As Jools and Beckett closed in, she released her hold on the reins and sent Nightwind around them, circling the moving horse and rider at a faster clip.

This so confused the quartermaster that he lost sight of his direction. Beckett felt his hesitation and immediately dropped down to a trot, then a walk, then a halt. Kim slowed Nightwind, ambled him up to the pair, and tapped Jools on the wrist.

"Game over!" she announced.

"Nice one," Jools said graciously, rubbing his wrist.

From his perch on Saber beneath the mushroom tree, Rob called, "*Nice,* in showing us what not to do. Stormie, Jools: can you two think ahead this time? Let's give it another shot."

Ruefully, Jools hauled Beckett next to Kim and Nightwind. Rob was about to give Frida and Stormie the *go* signal when he glanced out to sea. "Hold up, troops."

The powerboat that Whitney had been driving had appeared on the horizon. Within moments, it neared and halted offshore. Jools tensed, transmitting his anxiety to Beckett, who danced in place. But nothing happened.

Then Kim pointed toward the breakwater and screamed.

Out of the shallows rose a beast with a domed head, bulging middle, and blackened skin. Groaning and gasping, limbs outstretched, the thing lumbered onto the beach—straight for them.

# CHAPTER 11

**T**HE HORSES SNORTED AND BACKED AWAY FROM shore, their riders gripping the reins for dear life. Ocelot managed to snatch at the bit and break away, carrying Frida, the least experienced rider, up into the mushroom grove.

"Uuuuhh . . . oohh . . ." the murky-looking creature moaned.

*Black zombie? In broad daylight?* Jools steadied Beckett while his mind charged ahead. *Mob, as yet unclassified . . . Possibly dangerous . . . definitely hostile. Some sort of mod?*

Stormie fitted an arrow to her bow and drew back the string, locking in her aim.

"Don't shoot!" yelled Frida, recognizing the invader even as Ocelot whirled around the fungus patch up the hill. The novice horsewoman gave up, vaulted from her upset mount, and ran for the beach. "It's Meat!"

Now Turner's features came together in Jools's head: buzz-cut hair, barely past skull length; bulky torso, encircled by blackened mushroom doughnut; antagonistic expression, peeking out from what-ever dark goo covered his face. It was definitely him. "Sergeant! You're back!" Jools said with delight, before he could stop himself.

Turner's clothing and visible body parts had also been washed with the inky stain, rendering even his tattoos invisible.

Stormie trembled as she put her weapon away. "I nearly gave you some unwanted body piercings," she said to him.

"What the heck happened to you?" Rob demanded. "And what's that dang rocket boat doing out there?"

Jools saw the whites of Turner's eyes flash as the sergeant blinked into the sun. "Can't a guy take a breath around here?" the dripping, panting sergeant complained.

As always, Kim put the needs of the afflicted man before her own curiosity. The horse master slid down from Nightwind and fetched a bucket of water and a length of wool. She ran to Turner and offered him a soaked rag. "Moist towelette?"

Having caught the familiar scent of the man, the horses had gotten over their fright. So had the troopers.

Everyone converged on Turner, and the drill was forgotten as they escorted him to the shelter to change.

"Ran into a shoal o' squid out there," Turner explained, wiping the sludge from around his eyes. "Seemed like they all squirted me at once."

"And the diamond?"

"The griefer had it on him, all right."

Turner carried on answering the troopers' questions, but Jools tuned out their talk. *Shoal of squid . . . shoal of fish . . . What else? Shoal, shallow. To shoal something would be . . . to* make *something shallow . . .* "That's it!"

He came back to the present. His cavalry mates sat at the table. Every pair of eyes rested on Jools, waiting for enlightenment—except for Turner's, which flashed in annoyance since the group's attention had shifted from him to the lieutenant.

"The Mystery of the Materializing Sand Blocks . . ." Jools murmured.

"You've solved it?" Kim prompted.

He grinned. "I've an idea how they got there, at least." He paused. "Someone, or some *thing*, is soaking up the ocean brine . . . with sponges!"

Rob pursed his lips. "Come on, Jools. Do you know how big a sponge would have to be to wipe up a spill the size of an ocean?"

"In your old world, perhaps. In the Overworld—or more specifically—in the deep ocean biome, highly absorbent sponges naturally spawn in ocean monuments."

Rob was still skeptical. "Then why don't they automatically suck up the whole sea?"

"Because they spawn wet. You need a furnace to dry them out. Then you can use them for stuff. Therefore, a sentient being of some sort must be wielding them from somewhere *out there*." He waved an arm at the watery horizon.

"But why?" asked Frida.

"That remains to be seen," Jools said, satisfied he'd at least made the first move in cracking the bizarre case.

"Then why are we seeing more dry land here?" Stormie asked, still hung up on the optical illusion.

The strategist was certain of the answer to that. "Think about it. If you soak up a marine block anywhere in a body of water, the whole will be reduced in aqueous volume by exactly that much space. Even if more water in the immediate vicinity flowed back in to fill that space, the quantifiable lack of $H_2O$ would have to show up somewhere. In this instance, at the shoreline. We simply didn't realize that the missing water blocks would reveal the solid blocks that lay beneath them— somewhere or other." He sat back smugly and batted his eyes at Turner. "Now, Sergeant. You were saying?"

"I was *sayin'*, that I got us a prisoner who might have the answers to all our burnin' questions."

This was good news. "And what *else* have you got?" Jools prodded, bringing up the topic on everybody's mind. "What about the diamond?"

Turner cleared his throat and looked away. "Well. Truth is, there was a little problem with that."

\*

The sergeant told them that he'd lashed his life preserver to the retreating powerboat. When it dropped anchor, far out to sea in a deep ocean biome, he'd snuck onboard. Then he took the captain by surprise and demanded the return of the battalion's loot. The gems—including the UBO's prize diamond—were spread out on the boat's foredeck, where the griefer must have been counting them. The two men fought over the diamond, but neither of them could keep a hold of the slippery stone, and it wound up overboard. Turner had finally subdued Whitney, but lost the rare red diamond.

His words rekindled Jools's longing to hold what was arguably the single most valuable item in the Overworld. It burned like lava in his belly. He began muttering to himself.

The other troopers processed the information in silence.

Stormie appeared convinced that the escapade could've happened the way Turner described it. Kim looked like she hoped Turner was telling the truth. Frida's expression was unreadable, and the captain's was downright distrustful.

Finally, Jools erupted from his seat. "Are we really supposed to believe you wrestled the stone away from old Whit, only to drop it and *lose* it?" He stared at Turner incredulously. "You've taken it! Admit it! You took it and hid it, and now you're sitting right there, telling us you haven't committed bloody daylight robbery!"

Turner's mouth turned down, and hurt—not rage—filled his eyes. "Well, that makes me real sad, Lieutenant. After my great personal sacrifice and . . . restraint."

"Restraint? In not taking the diamond for yourself?" Stormie said.

"That's right," Turner answered. "Had it in my hot, little hand, too."

"Then how did it leave your hand?" Rob grilled him.

Turner said innocently, "There was a . . . tussle. Other guy went for it. One thing led to another, and the stone just kinda . . . sank. Dead away."

Jools could picture the diamond flying through the air like a scarlet prism. It would've caught the sunlight, casting deep red rays, and then hit the water, floating for an instant, before finally submerging into the cloudy deep.

"And you're telling us you didn't go after it?" Jools asked.

"You *didn't* pocket it," Rob continued, disbelieving, "and come back and tell us otherwise?"

Kim looked pleadingly at Turner, begging him to be truthful.

But it was Frida who said, "He couldn't have done that."

Rob eyed her, clearly questioning how she could know what happened.

"He couldn't have done that, sir," she repeated, "because Turner can't swim."

This sank in. Stormie finally said softly, "And the ocean is deep."

Now the sergeant came to his own defense. "Don't get me wrong. I'll wade in water up to my knees. And I'll paddle around on top. But I ain't goin' in the deep end without a boatload of potions and a dry towel waitin' for me when I get out." The tattooed mercenary had never come clean about the extent of his aqua phobia before.

"Then you *didn't* take the gemstone!" Kim exclaimed.

"Doesn't mean he didn't want to," Jools mumbled.

"Hey, pal. Speak for yourself." Turner gave the quartermaster a knowing look.

*He's onto me! Not that I would really stoop so low as to abscond with UBO property . . . or would I?* Jools had never felt such a strong pull toward riches. This must be how chronic gamblers felt. He suddenly had insight into Turner's guiding philosophy. *I see how a man might cross the line for such treasure,* he thought. Then, the next second, he added, *but I don't want to* be *that man.*

Turner grunted. "Ain't somebody gonna ask me about that boat out there? And the valuable prisoner that I single-handedly brought in?"

No one needed to. The sergeant detailed what had taken place after the scuffle over inventory. Turner discovered, as Jools had said, that the other player was all talk and no action. "Seemed to know you, though. Said he'd killed you once. An' that there's reason enough to get a love letter from me," Turner growled.

Jools's eyebrows shot up.

"You killed him?" Frida asked.

"Just acted like I might. Thought he'd have some useful information." Turner blew out a breath. "Turns out the guy's got so many cheats enabled, torture was . . . less effective a threat than usual. So, I just knocked him out and tied him up. Rifled through his stuff." He glanced at Jools. "You'll like this: he's got Bluedog and Rafe on his Friends list."

Jools nodded soberly. "Doesn't surprise me. Old Whit is the lad I told you went barmy for loot when we first started playing. Judging by his mode of transportation, and his modus operandi, he's continued his sorry ways and lost every shred of a conscience."

"What should we do with him?" Rob asked.

"You're asking me?" Jools tugged at the cuffs of his tweed jacket. "If it were up to me, I'd sling him from the yardarm."

"Whatever that is," Turner muttered. "Does it have tats?"

Jools looked at him. "It's not an arm, per se. It's part of a ship. It—never mind. What we *should* do is find out how much Whit knows . . . and whether he can point us toward that diamond."

Turner folded his decorated arms. "Now yer talkin'."

"Someone better go tow that rig in to shore," Stormie suggested.

"Jools?" Rob said.

"Aye, aye, Captain." The quartermaster nodded in anticipation and spoke with a note of malice in his voice. "It'll be jolly good to see my old mate again."

\*

IN A PAST LIFE

*Babysitting. As usual.* With Dad away on a business trip, Mum had slipped off to her habitual card playing tournament, leaving poor Jools to nanny little Ian. The boy was a nine-year-old ticking time bomb. The only way to defuse him was to keep him busy—which didn't make for a relaxing after-school break before hitting the homework and then the pillow.

It wouldn't be so bad entertaining His Royal Highness if it weren't for the oppressive rules that went along with the chore. While Mum seemed to have no guiding regulations for herself, the boys' after-school laws in her absence were many: *No raiding the icebox. Only one hour of television or online gaming. No going out, and—worst of all—no chums allowed.* That especially meant girls, or he and Jaspreet would be hanging out right now doing something fun, like working on their Mathlete problems.

"Joolsy!" Ian's reedy voice pierced his brother's pouting reverie. "I want a biscuit. *Now.*"

"You've already eaten a half dozen. You don't need another." *Or it'll mean my neck.*

"I'm having it!" Ian stubbornly insisted. Jools knew it was either let him, or take him to the mat. He didn't argue. Yet.

Jools sighed. He was beastly hungry. On Wednesdays, the school refectory served its horrific version of *Boeuf Bourguignon*—as though using a French name made the gristly beef in lumpy gravy more delicious. He'd taken a few bites before creating a replica of Warwick Castle out of the mess and snapping a picture of it, which he posted on one of his social media channels.

What he really wanted to do now was work on the extremely detailed Lego fortress he was building—and to nibble on crisps until he was blue in the face. This satisfying pastime could only be made more rewarding by sharing it with a couple of close friends. But, given the household rules, that scenario was totally off-limits.

His cell phone rang. He reached for it immediately. The police car siren ringtone Jools had selected made every call seem urgent. The number ID showed a call from his mate, Speed.

Jools answered. "Speak."

"Oi."

"Oi."

"Up?"

"Bug."

"Over?"

"Nah."

"Twerp."

"Later."

Jools hung up. He could tell Speed thought him a ninny for staying home again. Speed's parents let him decide how to spend his free time, so he filled it by pursuing his latest mania. Sometimes he asked Jools along for the ride. Last month, it was indoor rock climbing. This month, it was a new game he'd become obsessed with. Jools often had to beg off. Speed couldn't understand why his friend followed rules that no one was around to enforce, and was beginning to wonder why, himself.

He half-heartedly called his brother away from the telly. "Time's up!" The lad had been watching cartoons since they'd gotten home from school.

"Inna minnit!" Ian screamed when Jools called again.

The cell phone's siren went off once more. *Number? Whit. Answer? Well . . . why not? Better than nothing.*

"Speak."

"Here's the thing, Jools. And don't say 'no' before you hear me out. You want to make some money, don't you?"

"Well, I—"

"Then shut up and listen."

Here it came. The next in a long string of daft fund-raising ideas by the world's youngest professional con man. If Whitney made it out of secondary school without getting thrown in lockup, it'd be a miracle. "What is it this time?"

"Cat food."

"Shove off!"

"I told you to hear me out. This is so simple, it's stupid." Jools could hear him chewing and swallowing something, followed by slurping noises. "We set up a booth at one of those fancy cat shows— out in the car park, so we don't have to pay for it. Every twit there will be a ready-made customer. Who doesn't want to buy the best for their dear pet moggy?"

*Me,* Jools thought. The family cat ate better than he did. As if to underscore his superiority, Mister Mittens crept up and arrogantly rubbed his oversized black-and-white head against Jools's legs. Then he raised his bottom in the air for a scratching. When the human ignored him, he gave himself a good scraping against the coffee table.

"Here's what we do," Whitney continued. "We mark up the price of a tin of cat's-meat to double the cost. We promise to donate the proceeds to some sad cause, like starving orphans with incurable diseases in underdeveloped countries. They'll sell like hotcakes."

"But how do we profit from sending a few quid to some homeless baby hospital on some distant continent?" Jools asked.

"We don't."

"I thought you said we were going to make some money."

"We are—we don't bother with the charity. We pocket it. The cat gets fed. Everybody's happy."

"Except for the poor, hungry children waiting for checks in the mail that never come."

"Yeah," Whitney said. "There's that. Look, I'll come over and we can draw up the adverts."

"Dunno, mate. Not really my cup of tea."

"You'd rather make peanuts for pushing a pram around all day?" Whitney asked.

"Ian's nine," Jools said. "He hardly needs a pram."

"Well, you're going to need one if you don't stop acting like such a mummy's boy. This childminding is sending you back in time. You're regressing. You'll be the one in nappies soon."

Jools felt the insult even more keenly than the advances of Mister Mittens. Whitney's proposal, however, was irrelevant. He couldn't go out. He couldn't have friends over. He couldn't do much of anything, really. Except . . .

"Say, Whit. Why don't you come over and help me finish building my Fortress to End All Fortresses? I should be free tomorrow afternoon."

"Better idea. Why not ring up Speed and Jaspreet, and the four of us play some hardcore Survival online right now? Mumsy never need know."

Jools glanced across the room at Ian, glued to the television set. He checked the clock. *Mum won't be home for hours yet.* "Hang on, Whit." Jools walked into the kitchen, opened the snack cupboard, and rummaged about. *A whole sack of onion-flavored crisps!*

He threw caution to the winds. "All right. You're on."

# CHAPTER 12

IN THE NEXT LIVES

**B**EFORE JOOLS COULD SAY "BOB'S YOUR UNCLE," he'd been sucked into the game and stood knee-deep in rotting flesh, somewhere in the plains biome.

"Yes!" he cried triumphantly. "Did you see that, lads? Two zombies with one blow." He wiped off his iron sword. "I'm going for three, next."

The words had barely escaped his lips when a creeper walked up to him, hissing, and began to expand in size. Green and white sparks shot off the thing. The last thought Jools had before not having any more thoughts was: *Green and white . . . School colors! Nice combo.* Then the creeper exploded, taking the novice player with it.

Jools checked the screen and noticed that his hot bar had changed. He tried to reset it with no luck. He messed with the Options menu, but succeeded only in changing his skin. He hit RESPAWN. Having just learned about the need to craft a shelter and sleep in a bed, Jools respawned immediately next to his still-living friends. "What happened?" he asked. "Where's Jaspreet?" He could see Speed smelting something in a furnace and Whitney stacking gold ingots in his inventory. But neither of them answered. He tried his question again, this time typing it, and received the following reply:

> **LordWhit:** ID yrself.
>
> **Ools961:** It's Jools, mate. Who else?
>
> **LordWhit:** Says Ools961—Dunno any Ools—whaddabout u Speed?
>
> **XPSuperheroboy:** looks diff 2
>
> **Ools961:** I switched skins somehow. And I backspaced over the J in the name thingy and couldn't change it.
>
> **XPSuperheroboy:** howdowe know its u
>
> **Ools961:** Okay . . . we three had Mr. Sutton as form tutor last year.

Following a few more exchanges, LordWhit and XPSuperheroboy—Speed—acknowledged him, but insisted on calling him Ools.

> **Ools961:** What happened back there? Something exploded.
>
> **LordWhit:** Creeper. Can't u read? U died

**XPSuperheroboy:** u didn't come back straight-away so jaspreet quit

Jools was bewildered but relieved. At least Jaspreet hadn't been killed in the fatal explosion. But his friends hadn't been any help. *Couldn't Speed have nixed that creeper for me? He was standing right there, petting a baby sheep.* Jools let this slide, but thought of a fix. He suggested a strategy for vanquishing hostile mobs that hinged on one player at a time being on kill duty while the other two pursued their tasks.

**LordWhit:** Gd idea
**XPSuperheroboy:** u go 1st

So Jools did. As Speed smelted and Whitney amassed ore, Jools valiantly held their corners. He managed to pick off three spiders, one zombie, and one zombie pigman—not knowing that the latter mob would remain neutral unless attacked. While he grappled with the crossbreed, another creeper hopped along and blew them all up.

When he respawned, Jools found his friends taking the credit, with Speed swiping his XP and Whitney grabbing the gold, string, gunpowder, and rotten flesh that had dropped.

**LordWhit:** Crackin good fun

**XPSuperheroboy:** whatz not 2 like
**Ools961:** How'd u do that?

But nobody replied. If this was supposed to be fun, Jools was going to keep on trying until it actually was.

**Ools961:** OK—Whit's turn

Now Jools would be free from danger while he enjoyed constructing various complex structures out of simple blocks. A fellow could get a lot more done this way. The arrangement was already working out for Speed, who had turned to fishing for experience points. Like a real fisherman, he wasn't saying much as he piled up all manner of scaly prizes, throwing back the occasional bit of junk.

Jools got to work, mining coal and other things he'd need for tools first. He'd filled his inventory and had begun chunking up cobblestone when a platoon of armored skeletons appeared. He paid them no mind, expecting Whitney to abandon his own mining to slay the lot of them. He didn't.

As Jools concentrated on laying a hexagonal cobblestone foundation for his fort, the skeletons literally surrounded him. They all shot arrows at once, several missing Jools and killing their brethren who were shooting from the opposite side. Unarmed, trapped in the center of the ring, Jools couldn't defend himself.

YOU DIED!
SCORE 0

Frustrated, Jools hit RESPAWN and rejoined his mates. They were a little ways off from the original shelter they'd built together, where they had each spent the night in a bed, locking in their spawn points. There was Whitney, stoking a furnace to melt down his gold ingots. There was Speed, who had now turned to sheep breeding to gain XP.

**Ools961:** Hey—thought u were on guard Whit
**LordWhit:** Busy w/gold
**Ools 961:** Speed? Some help here?
**XPSuperheroboy**: Busy w/ sheep

Jools took another turn at monster slaying. And another. He lost track of how many times he'd died and respawned. When it became clear that the division of labor meant that he labored while the others divided his loot, he thought of signing off. Just then, his mum came home.

She must have found the crisps missing, the Internet connection busy, and Ian doing who-knew-what, all at once. The resulting shriek heard 'round the world ripped through Jools's ears and made his nose hairs stand on end. "Jools, the third! You get down here this minute and give Mister Mittens his flea bath!" she ordered.

This was the last straw.

The cat's fleas were not his problem. All he'd wanted was a quiet afternoon of multiplayer gaming with his friends, accompanied by a nutritious snack, while his little brother stayed out of trouble watching cartoons. *Is that so much to ask?*

Jools didn't think so. He hit RESPAWN again.

*

When he reentered play this time, Speed and Whitney were nowhere to be found. *They must be off trading in the village. Their beds are still here, along with the chest of junk that Speed fished out of the drink. And my stuff that they took! They'll be back.*

Jools waited, but they didn't reappear. The nightly moans and bone clacking began, and he had to fend off a gaggle of chicken jockeys before shutting himself up in the shelter for the night. He sat around, alone, looking at the torchlight. He hummed a bit, got bored, and notched more cobblestone out of a tunnel in the floor. "This is most decidedly *not* fun," he groused as the sun came up.

There was nothing for it but to set out in search of his missing mates. Jools was beginning to worry. "I hope they're all right," he said, eyeing his inventory and health bar and wondering how long he'd survive this time. His weapons were old and of poor quality. His health bar was full, but he had hardly any food put aside. He swiped his stone sword at a passing rabbit. The blade broke off and the bunny hopped away.

*Where are they?* he asked himself as he trudged across the plains. He tried engaging the two schoolmates on chat, but got no response. His quest bled over the days and nights as he crossed from the plains, through a couple of forests, and, finally onto a mountainous savanna. Hunting food, building and lighting nightly shelters, and defending himself from the hostiles he encountered before turning in at night were all he could manage. His inventory was low, his patience near its end.

But as he came up over a five-block rise, he spied a player he recognized near a cavern entrance across the hillside. The miner's dark skin was decorated with a flame design—Speed! Drawing closer, Jools noticed that his friend's experience bar was nearly full. Speed's XP level had increased tenfold since the last time they'd met. So, Speed was having a cracking good time. *What's not to like, indeed,* Jools thought bitterly.

**Ools61:** Oi. Thought u were AFK.

**XPSuperheroboy:** still here—leveling up

**Ools61:** Whit?

**XSuperheroboy:** tag team gold mining—he gets loot—i get xp

**Ools61:** Let me in on it.

**XPSuperheroboy:** sure cmon up

The terrain seemed to rise as high as the clouds. An unseen lake at the top of the mountain spilled lava over the side in a dramatic plume of molten liquid. Switchbacks carved out of the cliff made it possible to scale the otherwise sheer wall.

Speed and Whitney had collaborated to more efficiently mine gold, splitting the profits. This satisfied Jools. They had finally come around to the benefits of teamwork.

As dusk painted the hills purple, Jools made his way up the steep savanna terrace toward their mine entrance. The cave opening was merrily lit with charcoal torches. Whitney stuck his head out of the cavern and waved. *About time.* Jools was looking forward to some company. Maybe Whit and Speed would have some extra supplies to share.

Just then, Jools heard a moan and smelled an unpleasant odor. "Uuuuhh, uuuuhh," uttered the zombie that had spawned directly above him on an empty shelf of dirt. Its green flesh oozed around its eye holes, running down its face in brown and gray rivulets.

"Beg your pardon," Jools said to the agitated monster. "Don't you mean, *Ooohhh, ooohhh?*" he jibed, knowing the mobster couldn't reach him from up there.

The smell and the groaning swelled. Now Jools saw three more rotting undead above him. *Retreat!* he thought, glancing down to see a half dozen more zombies crawling toward him from the valley floor. *Press on!* he told himself, deciding to head for a ledge behind the lava-fall that might offer protection.

"Guys!" he called, hoping Speed and Whit would hear him. This was no time for texting.

"Ooohhh, ooohhh, uuuuhh," groaned the zombies above him.

"*Uuuuhh . . . uuuuhh!*" The gang below gestured wildly, losing a few limbs.

It wasn't too hard to figure out that Jools was the object of the monsters' heated conversation. The two factions appeared to be fighting over him, arguing about whether to eat him, save him for later, or transform him into one of their own.

With a surge of adrenaline, Jools dug his fingernails into the cliffside, thankful that he'd joined Speed at the rock climbing gym a few times. He reached the empty ledge, pulled out an iron shovel, and waved it at the oncoming hostiles. If they weren't damaged by tumbling lava, he'd pick them off one at a time. It would be easy enough to clonk them on the head as they reached the ledge, killing them instantly or shoving them to their deaths.

"Bring it on, you one-armed wonders!" he taunted. He hoped Whit and Speed were watching his brave stand.

The hungry zombies continued toward Jools, sandwiching him in the tiny hollow behind the lava stream. One irate mobster swiped at him. As Jools knocked the creature in its gaping mouth, his worn shovel broke in two. Both parts were swept away by hot lava.

Panic made it hard for Jools to breathe. He pulled the only remaining tool from his inventory—a wooden pickaxe—and checked himself. He'd nearly waved it right into the lava stream, which would have burnt it away to nothing.

"Guys!" he yelled for his friends again.

Another zombie tried to reach past the lava flow with an iron sword. Jools parried with his pickaxe, but the wood was no match for the strength of the undead and the metal blade. This time, Jools was left holding one end of the broken tool.

"Jools, old man," Whitney called. "Where are you?"

*Help, at last!* "Over here!" he screamed. "Behind the lava-fall!" Jools waved his axe stump frantically.

There was a pause. "Just let me get this last bit of gold. . . ."

But the armed zombie snarled and drooled from the cliffside, and Jools was fresh out of tools and weapons.

*Run? Stuck in a hole behind burning lava. Punch? Probably hurt hand, followed by rest of body. Jump?* He looked down. It was a very long way down to the dirt floor of the valley. *Fall damage probability: one hundred percent.*

The only softer place to land was in a bubbling pool of molten rock, far below. With no alternative, Jools shut his eyes and jumped.

*

IN THE PRESENT LIFE

*That's what comes of socializing with men of few morals,* Jools thought, as he looked back on his initiation into Survival play. His choice between a zombie, a rock, and a hard place had ended in a spectacular death, which he assumed was savored—or ignored—by his so-called mates. *They could've tossed me a sword . . . or an axe . . . or a bloody stone block—something.*

But with no better treatment awaiting him at home, Jools had chosen to remain in the game and make his way through the Overworld, seeking his fortune. He'd eventually gotten the hang of multitasking. He became adept at all the necessary survival skills: hunting and gathering, building mob-proof shelters, trading, fighting, and navigating the terrain. Once he'd found the right transportation—Beckett—and social connections, it was only a matter of time before he made a name for himself. High-powered people in need of solutions hired him to do what he did best: determine the most efficient way to get from point A to point B—metaphorically speaking.

Life as a detail consultant wasn't all bread and roses, but it was a living. And it kept Jools's mind occupied. Working out successful strategies—many of them in life or death situations—brought him in contact with all different sorts. Jools winced as he recalled some of the people he'd met in the course of his work. Some walked upright, while others virtually crawled on their bellies like the worms they were. Some players paid well, most paid willingly, and a few stiffed him.

Jools climbed back into the *Done Deal*, alone this time. "What a crazy job," he mumbled to himself as he took to the seas once more, to reunite with his old ex-friend Whitney and his rocket boat. "But, then, what's my alternative?" Composing high-level strategies was good work when Jools could get it. The truth was, it was tough to make a living in Survival mode, if a fellow didn't cheat.

Jools thought it over. He could've left the game, gone back home, and saved himself the aggravation and uncertainty of his freelance career. There were only two reasons he kept going: One, he was really, really good at it; and two, he didn't know how to do anything else.

# CHAPTER 13

**A**LTHOUGH IT WOULD'VE BEEN QUICKER AND easier to tie off the *Done Deal* and sail the powerboat back himself, Jools chose to abide by the unspoken rules of the battalion's code. Rob had never demanded it, but each of the six cavalry troopers had personally vowed to stay vanilla whenever possible. Cheats were out. Mods were scorned. If players couldn't make it in vanilla—the troopers all believed—they didn't deserve to play. Besides, towing Whitney's vessel to shore would really grind his gears.

So, Jools left the dishonest player trussed up and gagged, and threw him in the bottom of the unmodified boat for the ride back to the island. "Oi. We meet again, Lord Whitney of Firth. How'd the gold mining go?"

The bound teenager stared back at him defiantly, his only weapons two flashing brown eyes beneath a shelf of straight, dark-brown hair. He wore a rumpled blue blazer with a crest on it and gray trousers. It looked as though he'd never left the game after arriving home from school that day and logging on. Jools ought to know.

"I think it's time you and I had a chat, don't you?" Jools suggested. "Looks like you gave our chum, Speed, the old heave-ho, just like you did me, right?"

Whitney blinked in confirmation.

"My fellow soldiers want me to treat you with kindness," Jools continued. "But they're not here right now, are they? Besides, your interaction with Sergeant Turner was . . . less than considerate."

Whitney made muted sounds.

"Nice of you to own up to it. And nice of you to give us this ace ride." Jools gestured to the motorized boat towing behind them, christened *Great Escape* in flowery lettering across its stern. "I'm sure it will bring a few gems on the open market."

Jools saw the expression he had hoped to cultivate in Whitney's eyes.

"If there is such a thing as karma, old friend, then you're exactly where you were meant to be. It would appear you were reborn as a cockroach." Jools reached over and pulled the gag out of Whitney's mouth.

"Now. You'll tell me what I want to hear within the next seventy-five blocks. Starting with who your employer is."

"Why, the queen mum, of course!" said the griefer sarcastically.

Jools reached into a sack at his feet and drew out a bottle of dark-green liquid. "Cheats or no, you're not immune to poison."

"Then you won't learn anything."

"We already know you're in cahoots with Rafe and Bluedog. You must be in the syndicate. And you lot often do the dirty work for Lady Craven and her underlings. What're you up to out here in the eastern ocean? Come on. Spill it." He menaced the incapacitated player with the deadly splash potion.

Whitney's eyes went wide but he remained belligerent. "You, of all people, Joolsy, should know what I'm *up* to. It's all about money. It always has been, and it always will be."

"So, it's to do with the ocean monuments, then."

"Oh, fiddlesticks," Whitney deadpanned. "You've guessed it."

Jools narrowed his eyes. "Liar. Eight gold blocks aren't enough for you to bother putting an eyelash on the line. What's down there that you want?"

"Your sister's diary."

"I don't have a sister." Jools shoved the gag back into Whitney's mouth. "Now, I'll ask you nicely for the last time. What's down there that you're after?"

Silenced again, information seemed to flit, uncensored, through the captive teen's eyes. Jools simply read his reactions like messages at the bottom of a TV news screen.

"You're . . . doing something to the monument structure. You're mining prismarine—no! Something more innocuous." He paused. "You're mining *sponges.*" Jools could see he'd hit home. "Then, you're drying sponges and using them to . . . what? Dry the interior of the monument?" Again, a direct hit. "But that's not all. . . ."

A cloud fell over the boy's eyes. Jools grabbed him by the neck and shook him. "What else? What've you got planned?" Jools saw that the question fell short. Slowly, he said, "It's not what *you've* got planned . . . it's somebody else. Somebody . . . *imperial.* Not the queen mum, though," he said, removing the gag again.

Instead of answering, Whitney said calmly, "You know, it's good to see you, mate. But you're still all alone. Never could get the girls, could you? By the way, I went home awhile back. Saw the old gang. Jaspreet was asking after you."

Jools's anger flared like a sheep set on fire. He grabbed the bottle and threw it at Whitney. It broke, and the captive player immediately began to lose hearts. His eyes filled with fear.

Jools drew another item from his bag and held a milk bottle out to his prisoner. "Antidote, chum?"

Whitney nodded and garbled something unintelligible.

"Then tell me who hired you to take the stone from us!"

Whitney stubbornly refused to talk. Jools knew he was protecting someone. The griefer was far too composed to be acting without backup.

"Tell me!"

As his health slipped away, Whitney finally gave in. He moved his head, motioning weakly for the milk bottle. Jools gave him a drink.

It took only a few moments to reverse the effects of the splash potion.

"Who was it?" Jools demanded.

Whitney coughed and said, "Didn't . . . hire me . . . to take it—from you."

"Rubbish! You couldn't have been targeting the pirate. He said he got the diamond from you. And you could've reclaimed it at any time. A blind baby zombie could've stolen the gem back from Black Lung Bob. No, someone knew *we'd* be looking for it. And told you so. Who?"

"Didn't . . . steal it from *you*," Whitney maintained, coughing again. "Was merely—recovering it."

"Really. The Overworld's most precious and rare red diamond belonged to *you*. I'm sure."

"Oh, I nicked it, all right. But I was hired to take it. Not from you—from the museum," said the griefer triumphantly.

Jools's mouth fell open. He had to admit, the theft had been brilliant. The plan and execution had required guts, cunning, imagination. The scheme was nearly as sophisticated as one of his own strategies. Jools's respect for Whitney had grown . . . even if his esteem for him had not.

*Complicated diamond caper: Bluedog? Rafe? Sifting, sifting . . . No. Not capable of authoring such a plot. Lady Craven? Negative. She'd use a minion to design it . . . who would send* another *minion to carry it out. L.C.'s current favorite: one sociopath and possible serial killer, Termite. Underling of hers with knowledge of electrical schematics? Only one name comes to mind. . . .*

*Names, names . . .* "Hey! It was you who told Termite my real name!" Jools concluded. "No one else, except Speed, would know about my dad, and my granddad."

A flicker of unease broke Whitney's defiant stare. The quartermaster knew he'd scored another run. This scum was in league with Termite . . . who had formed an alliance with Lady Craven and her imperial army of the undead. Both griefer bosses considered freedom their enemy. It looked as though the two planned to use the sea to take control of the land and all its inhabitants. *Not on my watch,* Jools pledged.

Now he understood everything. "Land ho, chum. Let's go meet my real mates. I believe you'll be directing us to your employer's hideout, Whitney. Or, should I call you . . . *Volt?*"

*

"Volt!" Rob exclaimed when Jools revealed his ex-friend's pseudonym. The battalion members had all gathered on the beach as Jools brought the prisoner in and then dumped him on the sand. They circled around the helpless young man.

"He's the slime who burgled the Beta project's redstone torches," Kim said.

Frida pulled her special gold and diamond sword and menaced the griefer. "You're the one who ripped off the pumpkin farmer for her gems and crops!"

"And fed her false information," Turner growled.

"*Tch, tch.*" Stormie shook her head, eyeing Volt. "Stealin' from an old lady . . . lyin' to her face . . ."

"Big woop," Volt said indifferently. "I eat pensioners like that for breakfast."

This only increased the group's contempt.

"It's worse than all that, gang," Jools told them. "You're looking at our diamond thief."

Turner and Frida lunged at the griefer with weapons drawn. Jools put out his hands and stepped in front of Volt to protect him. "Let's not be hasty!" He urged his friends to lower their blades. "This pile of soon-to-be rotten flesh is going to lead us straight to Termite's nest. Then, you may do with him as you please."

Turner played with his twin diamond axes, twirling them like batons. "I know what I'm gonna do. I'ma rain on his parade."

"Any enemy of the UBO is a *double* enemy of ours," Kim said ferociously.

Volt regarded the small, pink-skinned girl. "Ooooh, heavens to Betsy. I'm petrified," he retorted. Kim pushed past Jools, drew back a foot, and kicked Volt soundly in the shin. "Ow!"

"Now you see that we mean business," Jools said. "You'll do as we say. Or you'll be sleeping with the fishes."

"Nice work, Lieutenant," Rob said.

They hustled their prisoner over to the pit corral and tossed him in with the horses. Saber approached him, snorted a few times, and switched his tail, casting a backward glance at Rob to let him know he was not pleased with the new guest. He stamped at the ground, making Volt cringe.

"You wouldn't dare keep me in here with these beasts," Volt protested.

"Wouldn't we?" Rob said and walked off, motioning for the others to follow him into the shelter. They gathered around the plank table, glad for the chance to relax for a few moments.

Jools's reputation had improved with this latest development, impressing even the resident weapons expert. "Way to ID, Lieutenant," Turner complimented him. "That Volt'll make a nice foot rest when we're through with him."

Rob was quick to reassert control. "He will be tried in Judge Tome's court, Sergeant. The UBO justices will decide his fate."

Turner pouted.

"We'll still need to produce the diamond Meat lost," Frida added. "As evidence."

Turner pouted some more.

"How'll we ever find it?" Stormie asked. "Talk about a needle in a haystack."

Jools laced his fingers together and stretched his arms out. "I've an idea," he said. "But it might have . . . consequences."

\*

Jools knew that the old Whitney and the new Volt would never have let the sea swallow the precious red diamond. It was more likely that he knew the gem's exact location. He would have let Turner think it had slipped away accidentally. "If you'd crossed into deep ocean," Jools said to Turner, "then the most probable target was an ocean monument, where the stone could be stashed in one of the many underground chambers."

"Who'd leave a thing like that unguarded?" Stormie put in.

"That's where the guardians come in," Kim said. "It's what they do. There're three elder guardians and a slew of littler ones in every monument. I read up on the subject in *Biome Geographic*."

Jools nodded. "At the same time, I'll warrant we find out what we want to know about the sponge bath that someone is giving the oceans."

Rob looked from Kim to Jools. "So, you're saying, all we have to do to clear up this mess and go home is to visit the monument and take care of business?"

"Not quite." Jools drummed his fingers on the table.

"Yeah," Frida said. "How do we persuade Volt to talk? And what do we do if we blunder into GIA headquarters down there?"

"And what about the horses?" Kim pointed out. "They can't swim."

Jools had already decided to keep her safe along with their mounts. "Clearly, our equine friends must remain guarded here in camp. As for Whit—er, Volt—we bring him along in chains for the dive. That way, we can threaten him with loss of oxygen if he gives us away to his boss or leads us to the wrong hidey hole."

"I like that idea," Turner said.

"And if we meet Termite?" Stormie said gravely. "Or Lady Craven?"

"Oh, we will," Jools assured her. "At the very least, when we remove the diamond, they'll find out. Probably let loose hordes of foul hostiles on our heels."

Rob's eyes widened.

Jools leaned forward. "Yes, as we make our escape, they'll come boiling after us like angry hornets."

"You don't seem too worried about that," Frida noticed.

"That's because they'll have flown right into our trap."

Now Turner leaned forward. "I like that idea, too."

"You . . . *want* to lead them back here?" Rob asked Jools.

"Wouldn't you rather fight them on our own turf than twenty thousand leagues beneath the sea?"

The other troopers murmured in agreement.

"We'll have them right where we want 'em," Turner realized.

"But we can't put the horses in harm's way," Jools said. *Or Kim.* "We'll fortify the island before we head out. And, Captain, I suggest our master of horses remain behind, for safety."

Rob hated to split ranks, but it had to be done. "That's wise. You'll stay, Corporal," he ordered Kim. "Let's not waste any more time. Quartermaster, pass out the shovels and pickaxes. We'll ring the area with bunkers and pit traps."

They set to work on chopping and stacking mycelium blocks, and gathering sand and gravel for suffocation traps. Jools looked in on their prisoner and tossed him a few carrots and apples, so he'd stay alive long enough to be useful. As Jools had hoped, Volt had to compete for the food with Beckett and Saber, the herd's worst treat hounds.

While Rob, Frida, and Turner dug and reinforced ditches, Jools and Stormie reviewed their potion and enchantment inventories. Kim checked all the horse tack and armor. The cavalry mounts had to be ready for battle at a moment's notice.

Once the plan was set in motion, there would be no turning back. With so much at stake, it was natural that the battalion would have to accept a high risk. That didn't mean Jools was entirely okay with it.

He found Kim under a giant mushroom, mending a hole in Nightwind's armor. "We'll be off soon," he said, trying to sound unconcerned. "Just wanted to see if there's anything you need."

She looked up from her work. "Yes—one thing. I need you to be careful, Lieutenant. This isn't your usual line of work."

It was true that Jools most often designed plans, not implemented them.

"I've become more of doer since I met you," he confessed. "Remember when I used to stay behind while the rest of you fought off the griefer mobs? Well, no more."

She gazed at him with admiration. "I wish you were staying this time. But the battalion needs you."

"And you're more valuable here. No doubt, we'll be fighting side by side before this ordeal is over."

"Always a pleasure," she said sincerely.

"By the way, I believe a little pleasure will be in order once we complete our mission." Jools took a deep breath, trying to calm his panic. "I wonder— and this is purely hypothetical—if you'd allow me to take you on a date. Say, next Friday night? You don't have to answer right away. You might think it over."

*Good mods, man. Could you have found a more tentative way to phrase it? Why didn't you just out and out admit you're a geek and that you have no social skills whatsoever? You ought to join the Lonely Hearts Club right now. . . .*

Kim set down the mended garment. "I'd love to," she said softly.

*I told you so,* Jools admonished himself. *Wait a second—she said* yes!

"There's just one thing, Lieutenant."

*I told you so. Here it comes . . .*

"What's that?"

Kim squirmed uncomfortably. "I have to be honest—I'm not . . . ready for a relationship."

It was Jools's turn to look uncomfortable.

". . . but I *am* ready for a date." Kim smiled. "How about, a trail ride and dinner?"

Jools relaxed. *Even a bitter geek deserves a little fun once in a while.* "I'll pick you up before the zombies come out."

# CHAPTER 14

THE NEXT DAY, KIM STOOD ON THE SHORE, HAND grazing Nightwind on a block of wheat and watching the battalion and their prisoner sail away. The troopers had marched Volt onto the *Done Deal* and hooked the *Great Escape* behind it for the journey to the ocean depths. Jools took one more look at Kim over his shoulder and reluctantly turned back to the boat controls.

Rain began to fall on the passengers of the open craft. Droplets bounced off of Jools's diamond helmet but spattered his face. It hardly seemed worth trying to stay dry when they were about to immerse themselves in the ocean.

"Which way?" Jools asked Turner, knowing he couldn't trust Volt's directions.

The mercenary had memorized his coordinates when last at sea. He shared them now with the lieutenant and Stormie, who plotted them on her map. In better times, she supplemented her income by selling geographic intelligence to interested parties. These days, she provided this information to the UBO government, for defense purposes.

The troopers shifted in their seats, unused to the extra weight of the diamond armor they wore. "Does this stuff repel squid juice?" Turner asked, thumping his chest plate.

"I doubt it, Meat," Frida said, "but I'm sure glad you guys recovered it from Black Lung Bob. Otherwise, this mission would've been dead in the water." Even the jungle-based survivalist knew that the highest grade of armor was a must for staying alive in the deep ocean.

"What about me?" Volt whined. He was still dressed in his school uniform without any additional protection.

"He's worth more to us alive than dead," Rob said, as though the griefer couldn't hear him. "But I don't want to use up our defensive stores on him. Corporal?" He turned to Frida. "Take Stormie with you and see what you can find on his boat. He must have some underwater tools of his own."

They hustled between the crafts and returned with some potions and a set of enchanted armor similar to theirs.

Stormie untied Volt so he could put on boots, leggings, and a chest protector. Taking no chances, Frida covered him with her sword. Respiration and Depth Strider enchantments would allow the griefer to cope underwater if he jumped overboard.

"Okay, troops," the captain said, once they'd resecured the prisoner. "Let's focus on the plan. Everyone confirm their order of go. Count off." Not wanting Volt to know their intentions, the battalion had rehearsed the scenario privately the night before.

"*Numero uno,*" Frida began. The vanguard would descend first to locate the ocean monument and scout out sentries.

"Two," Turner said.

Stormie raised a hand. "And three." She and Turner would engage any waiting hostiles to clear the way for the others, while Frida entered the monument.

"Four," Jools said, keeping his eyes on the water directly before him. The steering on the *Done Deal* was not all that precise. Once down under, Jools would guide the file of explorers through the monument maze, in search of their treasure.

The cavalry commander clapped his hands together. "Five and six," he said, indicating his part in escorting the prisoner to his destination. If the opportunity arose, they planned to exchange Volt for the red diamond. "Ready as we'll ever be, folks. Let 'er buck."

Even clothed in diamond armor, Rob's cowboy roots still showed.

Jools had sewn up the remainder of the plan based on the threats they anticipated. Drowning was not a pleasant way to regain one's spawn point, so they towed Volt's speedboat along, in case something happened to their own vessel. Once inside the monument, Frida would create air pockets where the troopers could refill their breath meters when necessary. Their armor enchantments would maximize their air supply and facilitate movement through the dense marine environment. Stormie had enhanced their blade sharpness, as well, since swords were more effective than bows and arrows at the bottom of the sea.

While Frida, Stormie, and Turner fought off any guardians or griefers blocking their paths, Jools and Rob would force Volt to guide them to the treasure vault. Then they'd either retake the diamond or negotiate an exchange. Volt hadn't revealed whether one of the GIA bosses resided in the watery dungeon . . . but they'd find out soon enough.

The rain had picked up, and gusts of wind sent cold sheets into the sailors' faces. *The better to stay sharp,* Jools thought, not that his tense muscles would uncoil anytime soon.

Turner indicated that they were nearing the dive position, so Jools cut their speed and turned over the controls to Frida for a moment, taking out the elixirs he'd brewed. The crew downed the water breathing and night vision potions.

"What about me?" complained Volt. "I'll need to be able to breathe and see if I'm to be of use to you down there."

Jools picked up the potion bottles Frida and Stormie had found on the powerboat and stuck them in his inventory. "These are mine, for safekeeping," the quartermaster said. "Your armor'll provide you air for a spell. And we'll be the ones to watch where we're going, thank you very much. You're just along as ballast."

Turner grunted. "Guy puts the *bilge* in *bilge water,* all right." He shoved the bound griefer with a Depth Strider boot. "Can't wait ta drain his pipes."

They reached the monument coordinates. Without discussion, Frida went over the side to verify their location. A few moments later, she returned and asked for a hand into the boat. Wind and rain whipped against her as they pulled her aboard. "Nothing there, sirs!" she reported to Rob and Jools.

The captain eyed the quartermaster, who shot an accusatory look at Turner.

"Memory playing tricks on you, Sergeant?" Jools asked pointedly.

Turner folded his arms. "Never."

Jools checked the numbers on his screen again. "Well, my info is spot on. This is the place . . . unless it *isn't*." His eyes drilled into the Turner's.

"Callin' me a liar?" the sergeant challenged.

"Is there a reason why I should?"

"Hey! I don't need ta—"

"Zip it!" Rob yelled above the wind. "You two can work it out later. Let's find that monument."

"But how—"

"Just sail on, Quartermaster."

So Jools did, putting the *Done Deal* into a spiral to systematically search a greater area. The others strained their eyes, peering through the rain and sea for any large, blue, solid-looking structures beneath the surface.

"Team!" Stormie said, pointing at the other boat. "Listen . . . look!"

Through the tinted windshield and the storm noise, they could hear a sharp beeping and see a flashing red light.

Jools interpreted it immediately. "That your depth finder, Whit?" He saw he'd scored, even though the griefer kept quiet. "This is the place," he informed the others, giving Turner a meaningful glare.

"So, I was off by a few points . . ." the sergeant mumbled.

"Vanguard?" Rob prompted Frida, who repeated her exploratory dive.

This time, when she resurfaced, she motioned for the rest to join her.

A rush of excitement, fear, and greed surged through Jools as Rob pushed the prisoner to his feet and they made ready to dive. In addition to the prospect of upstaging his former friend and nemesis, Jools felt a burning need to reclaim the valuable prize that had twice slipped through their fingers. What he would do with it once he got it, he wasn't sure.

He renewed his pledge: *That diamond is mine.*

*

As Frida hung onto the side of the boat, Stormie and Turner checked their weapons, preparing to enter the water. Stormie gave Jools and Rob the thumbs-up, and slipped over the side.

"All set, Meat?" Jools asked Turner. "Time to go off the deep end." He held his nose and pantomimed jumping.

The sergeant had been strictly avoiding the topic. "Got my potions and enchantments, don't I?" Turner grumbled, failing to cover his anxiety.

To make up for his goading, Jools gestured at a length of wool he'd stuffed up under the bow. "Your dry towel," he remarked. "For when we get back."

This vote of confidence seemed to help. Turner set his lips, pillar jumped, and cannonballed over the side of the boat.

Jools checked the time and ticked off the passage of five minutes. The time window would allow the advance guard to seek out and destroy any nearby hostiles before the rear guard brought the griefer down below. As the minutes passed, Jools got more wound up.

"I can't see them, Captain," he said to Rob. "How do you think they're doing?"

Rob just shrugged.

Volt spoke up. "I'll wager they've met elder guardian number one, and their remains are being devoured by elder guardians number two and three."

He certainly came off as cool for a man who was helpless and about to be used as a human bribe. Jools took this to mean that there was a griefer contingent down there, ready to defend him or to direct the resident guardians to do so. He gave Rob a hand signal they'd devised—a closed fist followed by a spread palm—to warn him to look out for two-legged hostiles.

Then the five minutes were up, and they were moving in file, as planned. Taking the plunge out of the rain and into the sea was like stepping into a Nether portal; Jools could only hope he knew enough to survive the unknown. He mentally tried to increase those odds.

*Descending . . . don't think about how far, just keep going. Breathing: Check. Visibility: not bad. Better than I'd thought. Down, forward, and look! Ocean monument, dead ahead. Whoa . . . Never saw so much prismarine!*

His head swam with the wealth of turquoise-colored stone, the most sought-after building slabs in the Overworld. *De Vries would sell his soul for this,* he thought.

Quickly glancing over his shoulder, he saw Rob and Volt floating down slowly. Near the monument entrance, he caught sight of Stormie looking out for them, backlit by glowing sea lanterns. They exchanged high signs.

*Still breathing, near the bottom, and . . . touchdown! I am on the ocean floor.* The sensation felt both entirely new, and somehow familiar. *Perhaps I was a crustacean in a former life. Moving, moving . . .* Now Frida and Turner joined Stormie at the entrance. They waited for Jools, and then the captain and his prisoner, to catch up with them.

Rob motioned for them to fall into line. Jools drew his sword. The captain already had his saber aimed at Volt's spine. They paused once again as Frida moved in to scout out danger, with Stormie and Turner following, ready to defend her.

The night vision potion Jools had swallowed offset the cloudy curtain of sand and seawater. He threw his head back to take in the enormous water dungeon. *It must be two hundred blocks high!* The prismarine palace reminded him of an Aztec pyramid, with its central vestibule and multiple winged corridors that clung to the ocean floor like gigantic arms. He knew it held a treasure trove of gold that would not easily be raided.

An unexpected movement came so fast Jools's mind couldn't process what his eyes had seen until he felt something strike his body. The waterborne block was all spikes and tail. He tried to scream. Water filled his mouth and lungs, rapidly depleting his breath meter. He doubled over, forcing the liquid out and recoiling from the hit, which had been powerful, but had not damaged him through his armor. By the time he regained his composure, two of his fellow troopers had moved in and dispatched the beast, which scattered some prismarine crystals as it faded away.

Stormie placed a hand on his elbow, checking to make sure he was okay.

*Breathing? Check. Intact? Yes.* Jools raised a thumb, and they pressed on, half-swimming, half-walking through the watery blue shadows.

Then Frida came hightailing it back from the chamber. Jools couldn't decipher her wild hand movements at first, but her eyes told him she'd found something surprising. Rob tapped her, urging her to calm down. She pantomimed dabbing at something with her hand and squeezing it out. *A sponge! The underwater room has been dried out!* Frida waved at them to follow her and see for themselves.

The suspense nearly choked Jools, even though he still had plenty of air. While he had deduced that griefers were displacing water from the monument, he still didn't know why—or what the effect would be. Again, he checked behind his back to make sure Rob and Volt were still there. They were; but only one of them knew what to expect. Jools gave Rob the fist-and-palm sign again, reminding him to stay on his toes.

They moved around a corner and passed through a glass airlock, which had doors that opened and shut automatically. Suddenly, Jools was breathing air again of his own accord. The entire room was an air pocket beneath the surface of the sea. It seemed impossible, and yet they were breathing. The wide, open area held a square platform, as though the space were used for staging plays . . . or human sacrifices. In the absence of water, the monument's base was visible. The floor was a mixture of gravel and clay blocks, just like the rest of the biome surface.

Visibility also improved in the unfiltered light of the sea lanterns. "Guys!" Jools exclaimed as he saw a blue-green aquatic hostile swim past a glass door, followed by three more. "Guardians!" he whispered.

"They sure as heck ain't no angels," Turner muttered.

Then the last one turned their way and activated another airlock. It was large and dull gray in color—clearly an elder. It swam in, then lost buoyancy and flopped to the dry floor. The elder guardian spied the players and turned its laser beam on them, dealing Turner immediate damage. He grunted in pain, but his diamond armor kept him from losing too many hearts.

When wounded, the tattooed mercenary got mad first, and then even. As the elder guardian recharged its laser, Turner lunged at it, moving swiftly through the dry room. Frida, thinking fast, withdrew a door panel from her inventory. "Here, Meat!" She tossed it to him, and he raised it like a shield. Hidden from the mobster's view, he couldn't be targeted.

Turner advanced until he backed the beached guardian into a corner. The hideous thing locked its spikes into place, squeaking in anger but unable to wield its laser. Then Turner lurched from hiding, stabbed at the mobster, and ducked back to safety. The group looked on in horror as the elder guardian lost just one heart. Turner repeated his movement, like a quick-footed boxer jabbing at a slower opponent—once, twice, again and again. It took more than three dozen hits to finally render a death blow.

The next moment, all the troopers saw was a pile of prismarine bits and a sopping-wet sponge where the elder guardian had been.

Turner's sides heaved with deep breaths. The sergeant kicked at the mob drops and snarled, "One down, two ta go."

\*

After a short break to replenish food bars, the group pressed on. In Frida's wake, the file of cavalry troopers and their captive moved deeper, toward the heart of the underwater stronghold. Some rooms were submerged, some were dry. Some ceilings were paneled with wet sponges. *No evidence of anyone in residence, though,* Jools noted. *And no response from old Whit about where to go.* The quartermaster dropped back to march near Rob, where he could gauge the griefer's facial expression and body language for clues.

Jools had already considered the chance of finding their gemstone in the gold sanctuary. On one hand, it would be ideally placed in the naturally reinforced core of the ocean monument, not to mention an area teeming with possessive guardians. On the other, a location that wouldn't seem advantageous might be more strategic. Unable to choose the option with the greatest probability of success, Jools let Frida continue toward the gold chamber, watching Volt closely.

All of Jools's experience told him to study his subject's line of sight, the set of his shoulders, and the tension in his hands. He did this during a few calm moments to determine what was normal . . . then he waited for those signs to change.

When Frida spied the central room, she called out. Volt didn't react. The alert group moved from a dry corridor to the flooded treasure room, with its elaborate pillared ceiling and dark prismarine walls. The griefer did not twitch, even when a large school of guardians and the second elder guardian swam toward them. *That's odd,* Jools thought, ducking behind a low block wall to avoid their lasers. He was grateful to have the support of the advance guard providing cover. The memory of Speed and Whit leaving him to battle mobs alone flickered through his mind.

He glanced at Volt, who crouched next to the captain. *That swine pays no mind to threats when he knows someone's got his back,* Jools thought. The suspicion that a GIA contingent must be lying in wait grew into certainty. Once more, Jools flashed a closed fist and an open palm at Captain Rob.

Frida, Stormie, and Turner made a valiant counterattack on the deadly guardian mob, evidenced by the muted, otherworldly sounds of swishing and slicing.

Jools and Rob didn't dare peek out from behind their barricade, lest the guardians catch their eyes and home in on their position. They had no choice but to wait for a signal.

At last, Turner's helmet-framed face appeared. He pointed his chin in the opposite direction, and they followed him. *I never thought I'd see Meat walk past a cache of gold without stopping. Heck, I never thought* I'd *do that.*

Jools's breath meter was falling. He checked Rob's and Volt's—they were the same. They'd all have to catch an air pocket soon if they didn't come across another dry room. Jools noticed Volt's shoulders rise, his back stiffen, and his hands in their spider-string bonds clenched into fists. *Up ahead . . . I know it!*

They rounded a prismarine-block corner and pushed through an airlock to find a heavy door topped with an iron gate. *Something valuable must be inside.* The captain motioned for Turner to pry the barriers open. The beefy mercenary used a diamond shovel to force his way in.

They entered another dehydrated room, this one sparsely lit by lanterns. The chamber was furnished with a bed, bookshelves, and a crafting table. Everyone breathed deeply to fill their meters.

"Team! Stay frosty." Frida's internal alarm must have gone off. "This lived-in look doesn't bode well."

Then Jools heard a papery sound, like dried leaves skating across pavement: "*Hyeh, hyeh, hyeh*," came a mirthless laugh from behind them. Every trooper recognized it. They wheeled around in their tracks.

There stood an armored woman with dark hair, her dark eyes regarding the group through white plastic-rimmed glasses. She dangled a scintillating red orb from a cord. It caught a shaft of sea lantern light and exploded with brilliance.

"Looking for this?" asked Termite.

# CHAPTER 15

THE QUESTION HUNG IN THE AIR AS THE GRIEFER boss spun the red diamond on its string. Jools was so arrested by the sight of the one-of-a-kind jewel that thought he'd been struck by a guardian again. He *felt* the gemstone's presence deep in his chest. *Has she enchanted the bloody thing?* He'd never been held in thrall by a single object before. *Must. Play. This. Right.*

"Why, yes, ma'am. We've been looking everywhere for that stone," Jools replied, mimicking Termite's über-calm tone. "How'd you know?"

Frida picked up on the tactic right away. "She knew because she commissioned the thief." Her voice showed no panic or plot as she addressed Termite. "Which is why we've brought Volt along with us. To return him to you. We know you're more interested in his influence than a lump of hardened coal."

"Volt's singular evil genius would be hard to replace," Jools observed.

"You've got me all figured out," Termite said. "There's just one problem with an even exchange."

"What's that?" asked Rob, who still held Volt at sword-point.

"Yes, what is that?" Volt asked. "I'd consider taking my old job back. Even with a slight reduction in pay."

"Shut up!" Termite snapped at him. "I have no feeling for you. You're not even a blip on my radar." Termite turned back to Rob and company, and said sweetly, "It's you I've missed. And the *influence* your continued unhappiness will have on Overworld control."

The veiled threat to the battalion and the UBO angered Rob. "You're outnumbered," he said defiantly, twisting his blade behind Volt.

The unstable griefer boss caught sight of Turner and Stormie communicating with a hand signal. Jools knew they were preparing an ambush.

Termite raised a hand. "I wouldn't do that if I were you." She pressed a button on the wall, and a section of floor opened up between them. From the cavity came the sound of angry chitters and clicks. Frida, who stood closest, jumped back.

*Silverfish! Termite's signature weapon.* She must have dimmed the lights and used a monster spawner. The lethal mobsters could easily survive in the dry room and overrun the players.

Termite retreated, swinging the diamond tantalizingly. "Now, Roberto, Jools the third, and the rest of you forgettable creatures: you can either have your pretty rock . . . or you can have your precious battalion. *Hyeh, hyeh, hyeh.*" With that, she turned and fled.

Once again, the subterranean criminal had left Battalion Zero in a no-win situation. If they tried to flee from the silverfish, they'd be toast. If they stayed and fought them off, Termite would escape with the gemstone. And, here came the scuttling arthropods—by the dozens.

"Troops! To arms!" Rob ordered. Their assault must be accurate and fatal. Wounding silverfish would only spawn more of them. But Jools hesitated, staring in the direction that Termite had run.

"Untie me!" Volt screamed. "Give me a weapon!"

Rob eyed Jools, who shook his head. The captain ignored the advice, quickly cutting the teen's bonds with his sword and tossing him an iron axe, which would be better than nothing. "Attack!" cried the captain.

Frida, Stormie, and Turner sprang to battle stations at the mouth of the pit where the silverfish were spewing out. The hostile insects attacked in jerky movements that made it difficult to know where to stab.

In a split second, Jools made up his mind. "Save yourselves!" he cried to Rob. "I'm going after the diamond."

With the mobsters already targeting the other troopers, Jools took a risk. He gathered himself, launched through the air, and leapt over the nearly empty silverfish hole. Without a backward glance, he tore out of the breathing chamber and back into the murky depths in pursuit of Termite.

\*

The special ambassador to Lady Craven had most recently resided beneath the rising city of Beta, the better to thwart the project from within. She had initiated many acts of sabotage at the construction site, using lava, a redstone bomb, and silverfish as weapons. It made sense that she would move into another underground lair, bringing with her some of her favorite defenses. Even as Jools ran through the watery halls, he watched where he placed his feet, hoping to dodge dangerous pressure plates and tripwires.

*Where would she run off to?* To Jools's knowledge, Termite never worked her own security. She'd go where she'd have the greatest protection—and where her foes would have the greatest disadvantage. The troopers had already picked off the first elder guardian. Then they'd neutralized the treasure-guarding mobs and their elder leader. That left one more great big submersible monster in the monument, and every report filed by previous survivors said the thing held court in the topmost chamber.

The top floor lay farthest from the monument's entrance, which was also its exit and Jools's ticket home. *So be it,* he thought grimly, searching for ramps or steps that led upward. The slower trek through the seawater-filled corridors increased his sense of urgency. There was nothing to stop the griefer from destroying or discarding the precious gem . . . but she probably wouldn't do that without an audience.

*Where the devil are the stairs? An elevator, a ladder . . . there must be some way up.* Gradually, Jools realized he was already rising. The monument had generated with naturally inclined corridors. He'd been so focused on moving through the unfamiliar brine and the slope was so gentle that he hadn't noticed it. All he had to do was keep going.

The saltwater made him tread lightly, while his Depth Strider boots allowed him to make headway. Soon, he came to a hallway that ended in an oblong, greenish pavilion that rose higher than the adjacent walls. Its surface appeared to ripple behind the moving water. *The top of the monument! Way to go, Jools!*

A pillared ceiling left the penthouse sides open to the surrounding waters, so the room couldn't form an air pocket and couldn't have been sponged out. *Might need more underwater breathing potion.* Jools could see more ramps, probably leading from different wings of the structure. *Note: escape hatches.* From one of these side corridors, a large marine life form floated into view.

Jools half-expected to hear the type of ominous music used in scary movies to let the audience know something horrible was about to happen. Although this was only his third sighting, he recognized the gray elder guardian and quickly hid behind one of the doors he'd brought to craft an air pocket. He peeked out to see the heavy beast slowly swim past the pillars, its blocky head waving to and fro, and its powerful, rigid tail acting as a rudder.

*Jools the third versus elder guardian number three: probability of melee success, not good.* The hallway was too cramped to avoid engagement. Even errant laser beams could ricochet until they hit their target. He'd be a goner. About the only thing he could do now was drink a potion of Invisibility and try to slip past the aquatic monster. To do that, though, he'd have to take off his diamond armor, leaving him vulnerable to extreme damage. The elixir would decrease, but not eliminate, the odds of the elder guardian tracking him, once he drew close. But it would prevent a player—even a high-level griefer, like Termite—from seeing him. For a time.

The strategist wrestled with his armor, finally removing and stowing it in his inventory. Then he pulled out his invisibility potion and a reed straw, and sipped the gray liquid. He gulped the last bit. There was no time to waste. He had to approach the hovering elder guardian.

It was actually difficult to sneak through water, Jools found, but he hoped the tactic would enhance his invisibility strength. It seemed to be working. He made it halfway down the corridor without provoking the elder guardian. The thing was huge, and it used one hideous oblong eye to search the surrounding water.

As Jools neared the treacherous sentry, he held his breath. Now he could see into the open-sided chamber between the pillars. Sea lanterns gave it an eerie splendor befitting another treasure trove.

Suddenly, the elder guardian's spikes snapped outward and locked into place. It had sensed him. *Evasive action! Now!*

Again, Jools used his dusty rock climbing skills to scale the wall next to him. The aquatic assassin needed a clear view to target him with its laser beam. It lashed out with its tail, hoping to hit the invader even if it couldn't be seen. Jools pushed off the wall, frantically swimming toward the pillared room, and dropping to its floor when he got far enough from the elder guardian to not draw fire.

There, in the center of the watery citadel, was a glass chamber. Inside, on a pedestal lit from above, sat his diamond, with his enemy standing patiently behind it. The glass-paned wall and the lenses of her squareish glasses magnified her dark eyes. She seemed to be staring right at Jools.

*Can she see me? Could be a trap!* Jools stopped and swayed in the water. The pull of the diamond and the push of possible danger immobilized him for moment. Then he found the airlock entryway, silently stepped on its trigger, and entered the dry room. It sealed off behind him. He hoped the griefer hadn't seen the transparent panes move.

"I know you're there, Jools the third," came Termite's measured speech. "You've upset my elder guardian."

His cover was already blown. "And we've killed its brothers. So, maybe living here won't be as secure as it used to be. Nice digs, though."

"It cleaned up well, once we dried the sponges."

"We know you've been planning to make this into GIA headquarters," Jools bluffed, "with no thought to environmental concerns." He moved slowly and deliberately as he spoke, sidling around the room to come at the pedestal from another angle. Termite would stand as far as possible from a pressure plate, which might set off an explosive charge. He crept away from the most obvious trigger point.

Termite sighed. "Once again, you've got me," she said. "Lady Craven and her underlings and mobs will move in as soon as the place is ready. We don't need to dry out all the chambers; just the ones we'll be keeping the monsters in."

"You won't finish that job anytime soon," Jools threatened. "Our army will—"

"Will what? Have you trained them to fight underwater?"

Jools flailed for control. "All we'll have to do is wait your people out. You can't survive down here forever without any air."

"Oh, yes, we can." She reached forward and caressed the red diamond. "We'll be trading this for a lifetime supply of underwater aids. Then we'll see who has the upper hand."

The griefers planned to mount a revolution from beneath the sea! Jools had never wanted to wipe out a player so badly. But he had also never wanted to possess something so valuable that was so close.

*Termite? Or the stone? Fight or flight?*

Jools calculated that he could do both. His diamond sword was fortified with the strongest enchantments. But Termite wore the very best armor. . . . If he were to remove her helmet, though, he could deal her a damaging blow, grab the jewel, and rely on a potion of Swiftness to power him out of danger. He'd have to use the pedestal as a blind, sipping from his visible glass bottle in the only place she couldn't see it—directly in front of her, on the other side of the obstacle.

Nothing could be more terrifying than crouching at the feet of the griefer boss who had killed him once before, with only a slim stone pillar between them. Jools panted, noting that his breathing meter had dipped. Hands shaking, he fumbled with the glass bottle and straw, nearly dropping both in his effort to hide them. He slurped the mixture and set the bottle down.

To his horror, it tipped over with a *clink* and rolled away.

*Hey! Distraction!*

Just as Termite spotted the empty beaker, he sprang for her with an outstretched arm. He locked his elbow and knocked the protective helmet from her head with his fist. In the next breath, he drew back his sword like a cricket bat and knocked her a horizontal shot. The direct hit shoved the griefer to the ground. Without stopping to see whether she was dead or alive, Jools swiped the diamond from its pedestal, slung the cord around his neck, and yanked at the sliding door.

Back in the watery citadel, he coughed and sputtered. He was almost out of breathing time!

\*

Jools dropped his sword and rifled through his stores to find another underwater breathing potion. What if he died now, after finally claiming the diamond? He found a bottle of blue liquid, but realized he'd left his straw in the glass chamber. Panic made him breathe harder, taking his meter down to its last bubble.

As his mind slowed and vision blurred, he managed to pull an empty bucket from his inventory and used it as an air pocket, refilling his breathing meter and replenishing the oxygen his blood carried throughout his body.

His vitality promptly returned. Jools dropped his chin to his chest for a look at the red diamond. It floated above his heart on its cord, every bit as beautiful as he remembered it. He picked up his sword and, keeping a hand on the cord around his neck, pushed through the water the way he had come. The natural downhill corridor would spit him out back at the entrance, he figured, where his getaway vehicle floated just a short swim away.

Jools's momentum and state of mind helped him stave off the three lesser guardians that confronted him near the central treasure chamber. They shot their lasers and shook their spikes, but he retained enough energy to draw a second enchanted sword, and used both hands to deal the three fishlike monsters the multiple hits it took to weaken and, finally, kill them. Then he continued following the corridor toward freedom.

Despite his love of fishing and his family trips to the shore, Jools wasn't much of a sailor. Yet, he had never longed to be safely afloat in a boat as much as he did now. At the mouth of the ocean monument, he replaced all of his gear in his inventory, took a few jumps against the sea floor, and pushed upward with all his strength.

Jools's hands flew to the diamond around his neck, stuffing it under his tweed coat as he passed by rock formations, baby squid, and bits of sunken debris in a blur. He burst out of the water, flailing his arms and legs. He looked wildly around for the battalion's craft. He could see it—a dark dot on the horizon—getting smaller in the distance as it sailed back toward the west.

His heart leaped into his throat. Despair threatened to sink him, right in the middle of the deep ocean. Then something hard hit his head and glanced off.

He looked up at the silvery hull of the *Great Escape*.

"Yes!" he yelled, grappling for the side and using drain holes as hand and toe holds to climb up to safety. *Aptly named craft*, he thought with relief, swinging a leg over the side of the powerboat and falling to the deck.

"Ools!" said a familiar voice. "You found me."

# CHAPTER 16

**O**LD FRIENDS WEREN'T THE SAME AS REAL FRIENDS, Jools mused as he caught his breath in the bottom of the powerboat's foredeck and stared up into Volt's smirking face. In fact, he thought, there should be a totally separate term for them. Both *old* and *friend* were too polite. They conjured up visions of acquaintances that had been left in the fridge too long, molding and shriveling at the edges a bit. As though it wasn't their fault they'd gone bad.

In Jools's experience, social history was more cut and dry. Drifting apart was one thing; severing a relationship was another. Jools considered leaving a person to die while playing at opening a petting zoo or even mining free gold as clear signs that a friendship was over. Without a shared bond, players were strangers at best, enemies at worst.

So, while he now stared into the face of his one-time friend, he knew LordWhit was long gone . . . and the griefer that had taken his place was his enemy. He would have to forget whatever pleasantries had once passed between them—if there were any—and treat this Volt like a wild animal. That didn't, however, mean tipping his hand.

"Thank goodness it's you," Jools said to the dishonest skipper. "You'll be glad to know that I gave your old boss a good trouncing. She certainly turned on you."

"Can you believe it?" Volt said. "After all I did for her."

"Funny how people can ask you to face grave danger without thinking they owe you anything. One expects some measure of appreciation in return, at least."

"Quite right," Volt said indignantly. "Cash is cash, but bodily risk deserves . . . something more."

"Like . . . favoritism," Jools supplied. "Loyalty, gratitude."

The implication was lost on Volt. "This is the last time I work for the GIA," he grumbled. "I'm going strictly solo from here on out."

"I know what you mean," said Jools. "I enjoyed quite a bit more freedom when I was a freelancer. Working for others on salary brings . . . restrictions."

"Oolsy." Volt's eyes showed the light of opportunity. "What say we team up? With your knowledge of UBO workings and my insights into GIA weaknesses, we might put ourselves in a plum position."

Jools's stomach lurched. Had the fellow no shame?

"I'd consider it," he lied. "If the money were right." Jools rose, dripping, onto the deck and glanced around. "Looks like you've done well for yourself. Wicked boat."

Volt preened. A light breeze lifted his dark-brown hair, which Jools noticed was receding from his forehead like a low tide. "I've quite taken to the sea," the griefer remarked. "Thinking of getting myself one of those captain's hats."

Jools pointed at the crested blazer the griefer still wore. "It'd match your coat." He pushed his fingers through his close-cut hair to help it dry, and then squeezed at each jacket sleeve, enlarging the puddle of water in which he stood. "But how did you escape the silverfish? And what happened to the others?"

"Your captain freed me," Volt reminded him. "I simply followed you out of the airlock."

*Leaving the troopers to fend off the mobs alone. Classic Whit.*

Jools had fled, too—but to secure stolen UBO property, knowing that his cavalry mates could carry on without him. "Where'd you go, then?" he asked the griefer. "I didn't see you in Termite's penthouse."

"I headed for the boat and laid low. Your so-called chums didn't stick around to wait for you when they got out of that mess."

Rob and company knew Jools could escape on the fallback vessel—and that Termite might well be pursuing him. They would've high-tailed back to camp, to warn Kim.

Jools sighed in fake irritation. "The battalion always was good at retreat. . . . Well, all's well that ends well, eh? What say you show me around this tugboat?"

"All right. I built it myself."

*With the help of a mod package and substantial cheats,* Jools thought scornfully.

Volt led him directly to the cabin that enclosed the command room. "This is what I call my sanctuary," he said. "Climate controlled, wired for sound, and ready to party."

Jools admired the cushy captain's bridge seating and the wood-grain paneling, which was dotted with photographs of bikinied girls on water skis. A drink dispenser sat in one corner and a cluster of uphol-stered furniture in another.

Volt walked over to a cabinet and threw open the polished wood doors. Inside it was every piece of equipment needed to record, play, and broadcast music and to capture and replay video. "Watch this." He flipped a switch, and colored lights began to twirl and shoot through the cabin. "I used redstone transmitters to improve on the lame entertainment center."

"And the boat controls?"

"State of the art," he replied. "Voice activated. Only responds to my commands."

"Brill," Jools complimented, noting the detail.

They peeked into the berths and galley. Volt then led Jools down a ramp, below decks, where he heard the subtle hum of machinery. "This is the beating heart of the *Escape*—the true evidence of my ingenuity," Volt said matter-of-factly. He gestured at a row of pistons surrounded by circuitry. "I diverted some of the power signals to my customized widgets—those extended arm thingies that do most anything I like without my ever having to leave the cabin."

Jools recalled how two of the auxiliary limbs had attacked their dinghy and captured its drops. "Handy. I imagine they operate from a central control panel."

"Right. They'll facilitate everything from an inventory transfer to a burial at sea."

"So, what've you got for defensive ops? Modified TNT cannons? Fire-charge catapults?"

"Oh, nothing as unimaginative as guns or flame throwers." Volt grinned. "Speed is my weapon. I leave every garbage scow on the water in the dust, so to speak." He exited the engine room, and Jools followed him. "So? What d'you say? I don't need a mate—everything's on auto. But I'd let you buy into the enterprise. For the low price of, oh, ten thousand emeralds. . . ."

"Hm," said Jools. "Perhaps on pay day."

"Okay, mate. For you, I'd go as low as nine and a half." Suddenly, Volt shouldered into Jools, knocking his jacket open. "Or how about—this!" The griefer grabbed the string around his neck and snapped it.

The next moment, Jools was looking at the red diamond in Volt's hand.

"Poor, daft Oolsy. I knew you'd manage to snag the gem. So I let you worry about Termite while I waited up here with the getaway car."

*Tricked!* Inflamed, Jools reached for whichever weapon was closest in his inventory, but the griefer stuck out a leg and tripped him. Then Volt fell on top of him, and they struggled a bit before Jools was suddenly incapacitated by a splash potion.

*Oh, dear. Feels like . . . weakness. Maybe some specialized brew.*

"You didn't think I'd really share all this information with you if I were going to leave you alive, did you Oolsy?" Volt said, menacingly. "I thought dying would hurt more if you were *green* with envy." He broke another bottle over the downed player.

*Poison! But that alone won't kill me.*

It looked like his adversary had an even more sinister end for him in mind. What was it he'd said his automated arms could do? *Burial at sea.* Jools tried to rally his strength. He was about to stand up to Volt and declare that a player who needed a modified boat could never make him jealous. Then, everything went dark.

\*

Jools awakened in a stuffy, unlit compartment, lying on his side, his hands and feet bound with spider string. Nausea made the pounding in his head worse. He listened. The faint hum of the luxury boat's power source told him he was in the engine room.

*Where is he taking me?* The water-tight boat had shown no gaps in its hold like the ones on Black Lung Bob's pirate ship. There was no way to gauge what time it was or in which direction they were sailing.

Jools took stock of his physical condition. He felt completely dry—so the seawater and splash potions had evaporated some time ago. He checked his health bar. He hadn't eaten since the snack break in the first chamber of the ocean monument. The three hearts remaining would give him some energy and buy him some time.

The poison, however, had left his mind numb. The usual rush to solve the problem of the moment was replaced by a mental shrug when he asked himself what to do next. *C'mon now, Sir Thinks-a-lot. Have at it.*

But no ideas came. Jools's thoughts drifted off, back to the school day when he'd entered the game . . . before that, to a particularly unpleasant family trip to the beach . . . and before *that*—to an afternoon when he and Whitney and Jaspreet had gone bowling.

\*

The tenpins alley was one of those all-inclusive, aren't-we-having-fun-now? kind of spots, with lane after lane of waxed flooring and automatic pin spotters, elaborate snacks, karaoke booths, and laser lights. The place bustled with movement and the clatter of toppled pins and clanking machinery. Once the three friends had changed their footwear to bowling shoes, Whitney took charge, as usual. "What'll you drink?" he asked, offering to go to the snack counter.

Jools and Jaspreet gave him a handful of coins. Whitney soon returned with jumbo-sized sodas, nibbles, sandwiches, and ice cream sundaes. "It's on me, lads," he said. When Jaspreet gave him the stink eye, he added, "Someone forgot to pick up their change."

*Yeah,* Jools thought. *Out of their pocket.*

They ate the ice cream first and then started in on their first frame. Jaspreet, who was tall and quicker on her feet than the two growing teenage boys, was a naturally good bowler. As Jools and Whitney worked their way past splits and gutter balls, she racked up the spares and strikes. Jools noticed Whitney's lips grow tighter and his attention wander as their friend won the first two games.

After drinking all the soda, they took turns running to the bathroom so no one would steal their lane and clear their scoreboard. They resumed play. Despite Jaspreet's better technique and Whitney's clear lack of skill, she began to lose . . . and he began to win. Now Jaspreet's brow furrowed, and her expression grew fixed. "Sometimes the pins get stuck," Whit ventured.

"Yeah. During reset," Jools pointed out, his suspicion growing.

Jaspreet gauged the tenpins, wound up in slow motion, and sent her ball hurtling toward their center. It bounced at the head pin and jolted harmlessly into the gutter. "That should've been a strike!" she cried, looking like she might start crying at any moment.

Jools thought his play couldn't get much worse, but after Whitney returned from the restroom, it did. He racked up all of three points in the next game. *He's rigged it somehow; I know it!* But Jools couldn't tell how he'd done it.

Poor Jaspreet tried changing balls, varying her approach, and swishing her hand repeatedly over the air dryer. Whitney continued to excel. Finally, Jools could tell, the girl was near the end of her rope. *I've got to find a way to crush old Whit.*

Jools said he'd be right back. He found the maintenance door and slipped inside, then counted down the lanes to their spot. The noise was even more deafening behind the scenes. Jools could see the machines sweeping up pins and dropping a new set down from above. With a little investigation, he found the wires that led from the machine into the wall, presumably resurfacing at the automatic scorer on the little desks at each lane. One of them had some sort of doohickey clamped to it . . . and the rest did not. Taking a gamble, he removed it and pocketed the thing.

When he returned, Jaspreet was sitting at the little desk, sullenly downing the ice at the bottom of her giant cup, while Whitney entertained a knot of players who fawned over his high score. He interrupted his conversation to demonstrate the form he was talking about.

Jools watched him miss the first roll completely . . . and then the second. His audience murmured.

"Why don't you go on and take my turn?" Jools said, and Whit did, with barely better results. The onlookers drifted away.

"Go ahead, Jaspreet," Jools encouraged her. "Maybe your bad patch has ended."

She sighed and retrieved her ball from the queue. Then she resumed her series of strikes, finishing the game with three of them in a row. "My first turkey!" she exclaimed.

"For the world's biggest birdbrain," Whitney cracked.

As they left, Jools nudged his cheating friend in the side and showed him the object cupped in his hand. Whit grinned and bragged, "Something I've been working on. It'll make me a millionaire. I can affect any score without ever having to leave my seat."

"Don't you *ever* do that to her again," Jools hissed and tossed the component down a storm drain.

\*

The memory triggered something in his foggy brain. *Without ever having to leave . . . without ever having to leave . . . without ever having to leave—the cabin.* Jools used his bound wrists to push himself upright. *That's it!*

He crawled over to the engine workings and peered at them in the half light. The moving pistons might offer enough weight and force to sever his spider strings. Of course, they might also sever his limbs, but there was nothing for it.

He pried his wrists far enough apart to produce some slack in the ties. Then he watched the rhythmic pulse of the pistons, waited until they raised to a high point, and shoved his hands underneath them. *Chonk!* The metal sandwich maker neatly sliced through the bonds. Jools whipped his hands away before they could be damaged, and then used his trembling fingers to untie his ankles.

On his engine room tour, Jools had scrutinized the configuration of redstone circuits that Volt had diverted to operate his "widgets." *If I can restore them to their default settings, those grabby things won't work,* Jools concluded. *All I have to do is get Volt to try to activate them . . . and then take him by surprise.*

He checked the engine room door first to see if he was locked in. He wasn't. Volt hadn't even bothered to swipe his inventory. The griefer must have trusted his paltry threads and potions to keep Jools out of commission. So Jools turned his attention to the circuitry and made short work of the rewiring. While he fiddled with it, he noticed a connection labeled DEPTH FINDER. The sonar tool probably helped Volt find underwater loot. Jools bared its wire and touched it with another live one. Then he waited.

Within moments, the boat stopped. *Yes, that's right, old friend. You've struck some sort of sunken treasure. . . .*

Jools saw the pistons try to engage, but their connections failed, as he hoped they would. A short while later, he heard footsteps clomping across the deck. By the time the engine room door opened, he was ready.

Volt didn't know what hit him when the hilt of Jools's sword met his skull and knocked him out. The griefer had tied a knot in Termite's broken cord and wore the red diamond around his neck. As Jools retrieved it and rolled the gem around in his hand, the day at the bowling alley returned to him. He looked down at Volt's limp form. "Cheaters don't deserve to win," he said with finality, slinging the prize around his neck.

The strategist dragged the unconscious player out of the engine room and up the ramp, back out into bright sunlight. He dumped the body on the foredeck. As Volt began to stir, Jools hurriedly tied him to a decorative cleat. He wasn't going anywhere.

Then Jools dashed for the cabin and located the control bar. He began to type in the coordinates of the mushroom island where Battalion Zero had camped . . . but hesitated. Returning to help the cavalry hold their position and take the diamond back to the museum was the right thing to do. On the other hand, he could just as easily sail in the opposite direction and cash the treasure in, living like a king for the rest of his life. He gazed through the powerboat's windscreen at the ocean horizon. There was no one to stop him. There was no one to tell him otherwise.

Somewhere in the back of his mind, though, he heard a voice—a petulant voice that demanded to watch just one more cartoon and eat just one more biscuit . . . a voice that rose in outrage when a certain brother followed certain unsupervised orders.

Jools's fingers moved from the keyboard to the diamond that hung around his neck . . . and then back to the keyboard.

He pursed his lips and finished typing the island coordinates. Next, in a marvelous rendition of Volt's voice, he ordered the powerboat to pick up speed. Jools hadn't listened to Whitney's get-rich-quick schemes for hours on end for nothing. *Glad that finally paid off,* he thought. *If only Jaspreet were here to see it.*

Suddenly, another female who was near to Jools's heart came to mind. A smile filled with relief, satisfaction, and anticipation spread across his lips. "Looks like I'll make our date after all, Kim."

# CHAPTER 17

**W**HAT DOES ONE DO WITH THE BODY OF AN *unfeeling, cheating ex-friend out in the middle of the ocean? Let's see: I could kill old Whit with any number of weapons in my inventory and—oh, yes—easily dispose of his remains. I could march him back to Beta to stand trial for his crimes against the UBO and let the authorities punish him. Or, I suppose I could force him to do my bidding, building the Overworld's most awesome redstone supercomputer . . . or letting me win at tenpins whenever I like.*

Jools shared these options with Volt when he returned to consciousness. "What d'you think? Perhaps I'll let you choose," Jools said.

Volt was still trying to understand how he'd come to be tied up, with Jools captaining the ship. "How about you let me go?" he barked.

They sped over the surface of the water in the bullet-shaped powerboat, with the sun at their backs. On a better day, they could've been just two pals out fishing. Instead, Jools was actually considering whether to murder his passenger or have him thrown in the stir.

"It's not like you're a saint," Volt argued. "Thieving, turning on your old comrade . . . leaving your girlfriend behind on a desert island . . ."

"*I* turned on *you?*" Jools exclaimed.

"Oi. Saw you tell your captain not to untie me, or give me any defense against those hostiles."

Jools threw his hands in the air. "Because I knew you'd pull something like this! And how am *I* the thief when you just tried to take the stone back from *me?*"

Volt cocked his head smugly. "Believe you took it several times—from the pirate, from Termite, and from *me*—"

"—the original thief," Jools interrupted. "And I had to . . . withdraw it from your bank account, shall we say, in order to redeposit it in the UBO museum."

"Which, I am so sure, you're going to do."

"I'm heading back to the battalion, aren't I?" Jools said, defending himself.

"It's a bloody priceless diamond, mate. Anything could happen. For one thing, you can bet your knickers the GIA'll be after you as soon as the bosses find out their loot is gone."

"Battalion Zero will send them packing."

Volt paused. "Might send you packing, too, when they see you sailing in on this modified pleasure cruiser with me at the helm." He let this sink in. "Might be they didn't take you choosing the diamond over their lives lightly. We might be sailing right into a death trap."

Jools knew Volt was trying to shake his resolve. Would he succeed? The strategist's willpower was at an all-time low. And there was some truth to Volt's speculation.

Jools's cavalry mates believed he would never use mods or cheats unless in dire need. But if they thought he'd taken the diamond for personal gain, then they'd think he'd stolen the powerboat as well. Their trust in him would evaporate—especially when they caught sight of Volt. They'd think Jools had taken up with him.

The battalion was already prepped for battle on the island. Why wouldn't they open fire on a supposed renegade? Jools had run off and left them fighting for their lives against the silverfish.

But, surely, Rob, Frida, Stormie, Kim—and even Turner—would understand that he'd been carrying out his part of the plan to regain the diamond. And, certainly, they'd believe he meant to return it to the UBO's possession. Wouldn't they?

There was a chance they might not.

"You say you've got no guns on this tub?" he asked Volt. "What about some sort of modified shields or force fields, or something like that?"

Volt nodded knowingly. "And you lot are *sooo* vanilla. Until push comes to shove."

"The cavalry and I survive on our own merits. But we do allow for . . . special circumstances."

"Like when one of you goes AWOL? I'd say you're facing a firing squad."

"No! Like when a mission is jeopardized . . . by a stupid clot I used to know!" He glowered at the bound man. "Don't you get that your actions have consequences? Don't you see how you ruin everything you touch?"

"Like my patented redstone devices and impenetrable theft designs, I suppose," Volt said mildly.

Frustrated, Jools snapped, "No. Like our friendship. Like my having a shot with Jaspreet . . . or Kim." He frowned. What *would* Kim think of him, coming in like this in a powerboat, carrying the griefer's treasure?

He couldn't wait around to find out.

*

The *Great Escape* hurtled across the ocean toward the cavalry's mushroom island camp. Jools had moved his prisoner to the cabin and found enough spider-string rope to cobweb him into an easy chair. He rummaged through Volt's closet and found some old underwear that, while not snowy white, would do as a flag of truce. Jools ran this up one of the decorative bow lines.

Then he pulled his laptop computer from his inventory and rang up the ice plains delegate, Gaia, whose secure connection he could trust. The camp was out of communication range, but the Spike City priest might be able to get word to them. Jools asked her to forward two messages: one to the captain, and one to Corporal Kim.

With that task done, Jools cut the boat's engine. He'd have to give her some time to alert the battalion or, as Volt said, they'd sail into a firestorm. Plus, he was starving.

*Supper time!* Jools had packed bread and chicken for the underwater journey. He helped himself to Volt's galley furnace to cook the meat and found some flower water stowed in a bottle in the cupboard.

"Oi, what about me?" Volt said as Jools returned to the captain's bridge with the meal.

Jools checked Volt's food bar. Keeping it low would make the griefer dependent on him. Throwing him a bone, however, might have a psychological payoff. He gnawed on his roasted chicken leg, acting like he was going to toss the bone overboard. Then he walked over to where Volt was strapped to the chair and held it in front of his face so he could get a few bites of the leftovers.

The griefer didn't utter a word of thanks, but Jools thought he noticed a shift in his expression.

*Good. I've done all I can.*

Still, Jools worried as they resumed power and approached the mushroom island. He hadn't heard back from Gaia. He hoped his messages had gotten through to the battalion. . . . There they were, assembled on the beach—some on foot, some on horseback—all in armor.

"Told ya so," Volt said.

Jools unwrapped him and pushed him out of the cabin and onto the deck. He grabbed the off-white shorts from their line and, sticking a sword in Volt's ribs, urged him to vault into the shallows. Then he followed him overboard and waded toward shore.

He saw Captain Rob motion for the vanguard to meet them. Corporal Frida approached—without a weapon. But as she drew closer, Jools could see Turner and Stormie fit arrows to bows from their perches on Duff and Armor.

Jools waved Volt's undershorts. "Don't shoot! He's my prisoner!"

Frida stopped, up to her ankles in surf, to confront him. "How do we know for sure?"

Jools looked at her—hurt—but he understood what she had to do. He dropped the garment in the water and pulled the red diamond from beneath his jacket. "I've got the stone!"

"How do we know you'll give it up?" she asked more softly.

He stared at her a moment. Then he pulled the cord over his head, cocked his arm, and threw the diamond at her. For an instant, it was as he'd imagined: the faceted stone arced through the air, catching the sun's dying rays to form exquisite red flowers of light . . . and then Frida caught it.

Without looking at it, she stuffed it in her inventory and nodded at Jools. "I'll return this to the company locker." She gave him a huge grin. "Good to have you back, Lieutenant!" she called.

*

Gaia's runners arrived as Jools was marching Volt up the beach. "A bit late, but no harm done," he told them, and invited them into the shelter to rest. He encouraged them to head back to Spike City. "We're expecting some old friends to tea this evening," he said, "and you might not want to meet them."

Volt was held in the horse pit again while the battalion discussed his fate. After hearing how he'd lain in wait for Jools to steal the diamond from Termite, Rob was almost sorry he'd freed the griefer to fight off the silverfish. "I thought he'd stick with us for safety. I really did."

"You had no choice, Captain," Stormie said soothingly. "It was the humane thing to do."

"I advised against it," Jools countered. "Some humans don't deserve humane treatment."

"That's harsh," Frida said.

"Man's tellin' the truth," Turner put in. "Them two have some pretty bad blood between 'em."

"Haven't you ever heard of 'forgive and forget'?" Stormie asked. "When folks can't do that, wars get started."

Jools crossed his arms. "He already started one. I don't think we'd be faulted for taking matters into our own hands."

"You mean—get rid of him?" asked Frida.

Rob said darkly, "There'll be no rioting here."

"I don't condone that," Jools said. "I'm just saying, as far as I'm concerned, the man is no better than a leech—a drain on society. He has not one redeeming quality, and I want nothing more to do with him."

Kim had been silently listening to Jools's tale. "You sound bitter, Lieutenant."

"I am bitter."

"I mean, you sound like an angry, old man who won't give a guy a second chance."

"Try, six hundredth chance."

Kim raised her pink eyebrows. "Volt may be a thief. He may have cheated you in the past. But you don't have to let that eat you up forever. I say, let bygones be bygones, and let the courts decide what to do with him."

*Who is she to tell me how to handle my old friends?* "You do as you please with him," Jools said stubbornly. "I have my standards."

Kim dropped her eyes.

"This matter can wait," the captain decided. He rose and set a few torches on the wall to counteract the failing light. "One thing's for certain: we're about to be on the receiving end of the GIA's wrath. That diamond is the key to their next step in Overworld control. They're going to throw everything they have at us."

*The diamond is the key . . . is the key to what?* Jools thought back to his exchange with Termite in the ocean monument's penthouse. She had been awfully forthcoming. Too forthcoming. "That's it!" Jools shouted. "Termite would never have told me the whole truth. She and Lady Craven must be planning something on a much larger scale. Maybe . . . draining several ocean monuments. Maybe all of them. And when they do that . . ."

Stormie's eyes lit up. "They might dry up the whole dang ocean!"

". . . forming an entirely new biome," Jools concluded. "Which, of course, they'd control."

Rob looked from one trooper to the next, process-
ing the information. "Interesting deduction, Quartermaster. But, again, it can wait. Termite or Lady
Craven could be on her way here right now. How are
we going to fight off their mobs and get our diamond
and our prisoner back to Beta?"

Turner coughed. "Glad you asked, Captain. I been
havin' some particular insights thataway."

"Well, thank the world generator," Jools spat out,
scowling at Turner. "Please, do grace us with your
strategic brainwaves."

The sergeant ignored him. "Now, listen. The enemy
has to come at us from the sea—no way can they
mount a surprise attack on the island. So, we can get a
good look at the hostiles on their way to shore. I say we
tailor our position to whichever mob comes at us first."
Several troopers nodded. "For instance, the beach is
ideal for silverfish slayin'. Them little buggers get loose
in the mushrooms, and we'll really have some trouble."

"Amen, Meat," said Frida, shivering.

"Head 'em off at the pass," Rob agreed.

Turner continued. "If it's skellies, those hills'll give
us the best trajectory for shooting arrows. If it's zombies, or anything else, we can skirmish from horseback." He paused. "Did I forget anything?"

Jools spoke up. "You did not," he said with grudging admiration. He grinned. "With a little more practice, Sergeant, you'll be giving me a run for my money."

Jools heard an electronic burble and answered the call coming in on his laptop—a text from Gaia. He relayed the news: "There's not a moment to waste, chums. Our friend, the priest, says a minecart train filled with mixed mobs just passed Spike City, headed our way."

Jools calculated how long it would take for the cart to reach the island. They had some time to prep and hit their battle stations. "It's almost too simple," he said—and then, more softly, added, "And Termite is far too strong." He looked at Rob. "Captain, we've got to be ready for an attack from two sides. I'll wager Termite and Lady Craven plan to double-team us."

"Mm-hmm," said Stormie. "Sounds about right."

Turner glanced at his cavalry mates with storm clouds in his eyes. "Only team we need is right here. Deep Ocean Six." He held out a fist.

Jools joined his mates in pounding it. He looked out the shelter window at the gathering gloom and said, "This is it, people! Bring on the night."

# CHAPTER 18

IGHT VISION POTION?" ROB ASKED.

Jools nodded. "Check."

"Bows?"

Turner grunted. "Two per trooper."

"Arrows?"

"Full stacks per trooper; reserves in central storage, paired with flint and steel in case we need to heat things up."

"Melee weapons?"

Turner smiled. "Boatloads. Still enchanted from our deep-sea dive." He fingered the leather of his dual shoulder holsters, which he wore over his diamond-armored chest plate.

Rob turned to Jools. "Everyone's already wearing body protection, except you, Lieutenant. Suit up."

"What about me?" came a voice from the corner of the shelter's common room. I'll be a prime target, too," Volt whined. Stormie had insisted on bringing the prisoner inside as dusk fell. She had quickly crafted a cube of iron bars to contain him.

Rob eyed Jools, who grudgingly dipped his head and brought out a worn set of chainmail armor from the company inventory.

"You should've worried about your hide before throwing in with the likes of Termite," Jools scolded, but passed the armor to Volt through the cell bars.

Rob looked satisfied. "That takes care of offense and defense for possible threats from two-legged hostiles. Any ideas for mobs with more or fewer legs?" he asked his troopers.

Kim raised her hand. "On the subject of the silverfish, sir, why not try a multi-pronged approach?" She described the iron tool that Swale had fashioned to pitch hay on the horse farm.

"A prong!" Jools said, sketching a long-handled tool with several sharp tines at the end and showing it to her.

Kim nodded. "I call it a pitchfork. With five spikes on the end, we can hit that many silverfish with one thrust."

Frida gave her a thumbs-up.

"Sweet," Turner said. "I'll craft a dozen right now." The weapons expert had learned some blacksmithing from his girlfriend, Sundra.

Rob agreed, and then continued. "What if we need more firepower?"

Everyone looked at Stormie. The artilleryman frowned. "Sad to say, gang, my lil' old TNT cannon ain't exactly Hercules." She leaned forward at the table. "Consider the terrain. This island is pert near round. We foresee attacks from the west, from minecart to barge to island—and from the east, by sea, from the approximate direction of the ocean monument. One small cannon can't cover the whole of it."

"What would be the best tactical use?" Rob pressed.

Turner cut in. "I'd point it to sea, as a failsafe. We know we can handle Lady Craven's minecart mobs, even if they're enchanted. We don't know what might come from out deep ocean way."

"I concur," said Jools. "Skellies and zombies are largely vanilla. If we assume that an advance from the eastern flank will be orchestrated by Termite, however, we can take nothing for granted. We must be ready to blow her out of the water, as it were."

"Which we ain't," Stormie admitted sadly.

The room was silent for a moment. Then Volt again spoke up from his jail cell in the corner: "I might be able to help."

Jools shot him a disparaging look. "Help tank the effort, you mean. All he wants is to cultivate leniency and reduce his potential sentence."

"Is that such a bad thing?" said the captain. "Let's hear him out."

Volt sniffed and drew himself upright in the cage. "What you need is a mechanism that allows for a turret sweep, yes?" He demonstrated with an arm firing in a broad arch. "And a rapid-fire repeater?"

Stormie showed interest. "That'd be a start. We'd have to increase the cannon's range and thrust if we're to repel incoming troops by sea. Is that a problem?"

The griefer snorted. "Child's play."

"That's not saying much, coming from the most infantile thief in the Overworld . . ." Jools snapped. "Captain, you don't possibly think he's sincere—?"

"I can read a man's strengths, Quartermaster," Rob said shortly. "And a certain First War cavalry commander once told me to write those into my war plan whenever possible."

\*

Battalion Zero's origins were evident in the ensuing preparation. Kim saddled the horses and tied them to a picket line just under the giant mushroom caps at the edge of the island sands. What had been a mycelium beachfront not long before had become sandy beach as the ocean receded.

The sergeant at arms distributed weapons and ammunition, and stashed the backup resources in a stone bunker. He had sited it next to the picket line, midway between the two likely enemy landing points. "Anybody runs short of blades or ammo, call for cover and hit this storehouse," he instructed the troops.

Frida would be stationed at the island's high point to search for incoming hostiles. She and Jools worked up a signal code that she'd flash with a redstone chunk, to indicate where to center their defense. Meanwhile, Stormie freed Volt long enough to help her adapt her TNT cannon to meet a potential naval attack. "Could be creepers, could be monster egg launchers, for all we know," she told him.

"Knowing Termite, could be a mod you've never envisioned in your wildest dreams," Volt said. "I'd keep an eye on that diamond."

Hearing this, Jools took Rob aside. "If something should happen to me, our communal inventory might be lost. I suggest building a bulletproof case in which to store our red 'star'."

Rob asked him to deposit the valuable gemstone in a locked chest and place it in a stone pit inside the shelter. Once they'd secured it, Volt was returned to his cage awaiting Rob's further instruction.

These tasks completed, the troopers were sent off to see that their horses were armored and ready for battle.

Jools checked Beckett's saddle girth and gave him
a potion of Swiftness, then handed the bottle to Frida,
who was seeing to Ocelot. Kim arrived, leading Nightwind. She held out a sugar lump on the flat of her hand,
and Beckett gobbled it. "For luck," she whispered.

Jools held out a palm. "What about me?" he mimicked their prisoner, only half-joking.

"You don't need luck," Kim said disapprovingly.
"Or sugar. You need a good dose of compassion."

He scowled. "Still hung up on the good-man
potential in Volt, eh?"

"No, not in him." She moved away and said over
her shoulder, "In you."

Before long, the cavalry commander called the battalion onto the beach and issued last-minute encouragement. Then he said, "This is it! Battle stations,
troops! You all know what to do." He put a foot in
the stirrup of Saber's saddle and swung up. "May the
horse be with you."

Frida scrambled up the hill to her lookout. Stormie,
Turner, and Jools crept across the mycelium terrace
with their bows and arrows. Rob and Horse Master
Kim rode their mounts to the eastern beachfront to
guard the perimeter. Then they all waited.

As Jools had anticipated, the mobs that Gaia had
spotted traveling by minecart arrived first. They would
have been moved from train to barge for the short

float out to the island from the west, presumably by one of Lady Craven's mainland minions. She'd tried that tactic before.

Frida had barely flickered her coded message to the troopers below her on Mushroom Mountain when the noises of the night mobs reached their ears:

"Uuuuhh, ooohhh!"

*Packetta-clacketta clack!*

Jools heard the mobs splash through the shallows toward the beach, and his bow arm tensed. The quicker skeletons would reach them before the slower-moving zombies could. Jools peered out from behind the mushroom thicket he'd chosen as a screen. Sure enough, he could see the whitish bones of the skellies washed by moonlight, their ragged ranks sweeping toward them . . . too fast—on too many legs. He fumbled for an arrow. "What the—"

Frida's shout cut off his question. *"Spider jockeys!"* she cried from the hilltop.

"No wonder they got here from Spike City so fast," Jools said aloud, knowing that the skeleton-spider combination increased the speed of moving minecarts.

Turner, watched nearby, setting his bow with an arrow. "Them things make my skin crawl."

Stormie hustled out of the shadows. "Better crawl fast, then. Here they come!" She opened her mouth and let go a hair-raising battle cry.

The swift and agile spiders must have been brainwashed by the sorceress, Lady Craven. Their course never wavered. Normally with agendas of their own, the spiders carried their armed and armored skelejockeys directly toward the three players' station, uphill.

"Squadron!" Jools called to Turner and Stormie. "Prepare to engage." *Big time!* he thought.

Jools tried to count the incoming spider jockeys, but left off at three dozen when he had to open fire against them. "Captain!" he yelled over the groans and jangling bones. "We need backup!" His voice carried, bouncing off the tops of mushrooms and ridges of mycelium. *Good call on this location, Turner.*

Suddenly, motion and sound melded into a horrifying display of GIA vengeance: Spider legs flashed and thundered. Skeleton arms quivered, loosing arrows that hissed through the air. Behind them all rose a surging moan unlike anything Jools had ever heard before. The zombies' cries ricocheted off the glassy ocean waters, distorting and swelling, announcing the approach of their tide of death.

*Thoop! Th-oop! Thwap!* Arrows missed, then found their targets. Some were Jools's, some were Stormie's and Turner's. A plague of them came from the opposite direction, but the squadron kept pace. The three troopers had never fired so furiously.

*Choing! Chwang! CR-ACK!* Jools overflexed his bowstring and broke the weapon's back. He faded into the mushroom underbrush for cover while he drew another bow from his inventory.

"Aaugh!" he heard Stormie react to a hit that got past her armor. She thudded to the ground.

"Private?" Jools called, even as he sighted on another skeleton.

"I'm okay." She appeared in the half light, staggering, but already aiming at another assailant. "Your mother was a corpse!" she snarled.

"Sergeant?" Jools wanted to know Turner's position.

"Over here." The mercenary had climbed atop a medium-sized mushroom for a better vantage point. "Try hittin' the spiders first! Then you can pick off the skellies at will."

The technique proved useful. Shooting their eight-legged mounts out from under them caused some skeletons to crash, tumble, and die. Others had to crawl uphill, making them easier targets.

Still, Jools felt their arrows glance off his helmet, his chest plate, his leggings. How long would the diamond armor hold up? How long would their enchantments last? His grunts mingled with Turner's curses and Stormie's taunts.

Another rumble arose—made by another set of eight legs. *Hoofbeats!* In rode Kim and Rob to support the flagging squadron.

Jools shimmied up a mushroom stalk to have a look. *Th-oop!* A skeleton's arrow narrowly missed his ear. In the next second, he saw Captain Rob and Saber run down a mobster's hairy mount and literally trample the pair into the ground. If Jools wasn't mistaken, Saber had a gleam in his eye that meant the stallion had taken offense at the lesser species' challenge on his turf.

A ways off, Kim charged Nightwind up a steep slope after a trio of spider jockeys that had locked on to Stormie's coordinates. The corporal had exchanged her bow for a diamond sword bursting with enchantments. She gained on the mobsters with her blade outstretched. In a dashing show of horsemanship, she legged Nightwind across the hillside, swiping at the skellies in a single motion. "Die! Die! Die!" she screamed, and they fell—one, two, three. This unbalanced their mounts, which slammed into one another and somersaulted down the hill to their deaths.

After some additional creative combat, the number of spiders and skeletons was reduced to single digits—if you didn't count distinct limbs. While the corporal and captain cleaned them up from below, Jools's squadron made a game of finishing them off from above.

"After you, Sergeant," Stormie graciously waved Turner toward a wobbling skeleton riding a stumbling spider.

"Don't mind if I do!" *P-toing! P-toing!* "Your turn, Artilleryman."

Stormie sighted a pair that had separated from the rest. She aimed her bow straight up and unleashed two arrows, one after the other. After long, high arcs, they rocketed back down to earth and met their targets.

Seeing Rob and Kim grappling with one of the last two spider jockeys, Jools said to Stormie and Turner, "I'll take this one. May I borrow your axes, Sergeant?" Turner pulled them from their holsters and handed them over.

Jools let the hairy black spider bound all the way up the hill until he saw the red of its eyes. As its rider locked on to the trooper with bow and arrow, Jools broke off a chunk of mushroom and tossed it aside. "Think fast!" he called in false warning. When the skeleton followed the movement, Jools broke from cover, stalked up to the twosome, and dealt them simultaneous death blows with Turner's diamond axes. "Mission accomplished," he said, returning the weapons to their owner.

But the cavalry troopers were too practiced to revel in their success for long—especially when the zombie lament placed the next wave of attackers almost in range.

"Quick!" the captain called. "Fall back to the supply bunker to regroup."

The squadron stumbled down the hill in Saber's and Nightwind's wake. Jools called to Kim, "Nice riding, Corporal!"

She caught his eye with her night vision. "Thanks." She motioned for him to grab her hand, and she pulled him up behind her onto Nightwind's back. Together, they rode to the bunker, buoyed by the victory.

"Resupply and mount up!" Rob commanded. "We'll have to hold this beach to safeguard the treasure."

"Uuuuhh. . . *ooohhh!*" The wails grew more insistent as the zombies caught the scent of the living. Answering yells carried across the beach.

"Jools! Captain! Can anybody hear me!" It was Volt, clamoring from his prison cell to be released.

Rob eyed Jools. But, at that moment, Frida's voice rose. "Battalion! Navy ship at nine o'clock!"

All eyes swung due east.

*Blimey!* If Jools hadn't known better, he'd have thought he was caught in some sort of world warp—one that let the objects from his old life into his new one. On the bruise-colored ocean, a dark shape stood out. It was a humongous vessel—the size of two football fields—with gun muzzles as large as tree trunks protruding from its massive deck turrets. They swung ominously in the night . . . until they were pointed directly at the beach where he stood.

# CHAPTER 19

THE CAPTAIN RECALLED FRIDA FROM HER LOOK-out post and ordered the other troopers into mounted file, except for Stormie. He pulled her aside and asked tersely, "Will your cannon take on that battleship?"

She gaped at the hulking thing floating in the bay, the product of a cruel mod and a sick mind. "Can't say for sure, Captain. But I'ma try." She ran for the shelter and returned a few moments later with their prisoner. Volt predicted the enhanced TNT cannon could strike the target—but how much damage it might deal remained to be seen.

"We need you on the front line, Artilleryman," Rob said, glancing over his shoulder at the zombie ranks advancing from the west. "Can you set that thing on automatic?"

"Better idea, Captain," Jools said, nudging Beckett over to them. "Let's put Volt on it. His life's on the line, too. That should keep him on task, if not on his honor."

Rob eyed them both. "Your call," he said to his lieutenant.

Jools rode Beckett over to Volt and had a quiet word with him. The griefer crept into the turret Stormie had crafted. Jools wheeled his horse and raised a thumb at the captain. "At your orders, sir!"

Frida was still a few dozen blocks off, running pell mell down the hill. "Don't wait for me!"

"Front into line!" Rob called. "March!"

Stormie sprang into Armor's saddle and took her place at the head of the file, ponying a riderless Ocelot. Duff, Beckett, Nightwind, and then Saber moved up behind her, then spread out to form a phalanx in no time flat. Frida came sprinting across the mycelium flats to jump on her horse.

The zombies steadily closed the gap between the western shore and the troops. *"Uuuuhh . . . ooohhh . . . OOOHHH!"* Their putrefying stench rose along with their guttural voices. Sitting atop Beckett, Jools felt like a death sandwich, stuck between the GIA's hordes and Termite's battleship like so much meat.

Rob had no choice but to turn the riders on the hungry zombies, putting the live guns—and the unreliable Volt—at their backs. "Battalion: left wheel!"

Although he was surrounded by his mates, Jools had never felt so exposed. The deadly silence of the waiting warship was every bit as terrifying as the mob's moans. The quartermaster placed a hand on Beckett's neck to steady himself. "All right, old chum. Give it your all."

The captain ordered sabers drawn. "And, charge!"

It was a good thing zombies had no knowledge of cavalry technique—or much of anything else, really. Rob kept the group in tight formation, and they galloped as one at the sloppy sea of zombies that spilled over the darkened sands. The advance guard of baby zombies came at them first, drooling past single teeth and waving gold swords. They were well armored beneath their diapers, and low enough to the ground that the troopers had a hard time reaching them from horseback with their blades.

Kim had a bright idea. "Captain! Let's make a pass at that pit trap!"

He trusted her instincts and ordered the file in its direction. The baby mobsters made a beeline for them.

"How about some candy, kids?" Kim yelled. She tossed handfuls of sugar cubes into the pits. The baby zombies' ghoulish eyes went wide, and they fought each other to get at the sweets.

"Yaaaahh! Yoooohhh!" . . . *bump! bump! bump!* They hurtled into the pits and fell to the bottom. This

*Nancy Osa*

triggered the release of a dozen blocks of sand from the trees above. The blocks broke, dropping enough sand to silence the wailing urchins once and for all.

"Way ta deal with a temper tantrum, Corporal!" Turner called from across their ranks.

"Incoming!" Stormie yelled.

The slower adults now caught up with the battalion, and there was nothing precious about this bunch. Jools almost wished his night vision potion didn't work quite as well as it did. He'd never get the image of ragged limbs, corroded flesh, and empty eye sockets out of his mind, he was sure. *And there's no potion to get this vile stink out of my nostrils.*

Again, the cavalry's training stood them in good stead. Their short-range weapons were more effective against full-sized monsters. As the riders cut down the undead directly before them, their zombie comrades tried to change course. In a slow shuffle, they barely split formation before Battalion Zero sliced away at another slew of them.

The melee's success, though, brought with it more danger: when the decaying monsters fell, their drops littered the beach. Severed limbs, rotting vegetables, iron ingots, and pilfered armor created an obstacle course on the terrain. Suddenly, Duff tripped on a chunk of something and broke file. This allowed the nearest dead-eyed mobsters to lunge forward into the gap—flailing, grasping, and stabbing with their stolen weapons. Beckett took a terrible gash to the barrel and skittered sideways, knocking into Nightwind.

"Easy," Jools comforted him, collecting the horse with his legs and seat, and urging him forward once more. A glance told him that Kim was okay and had brought Nightwind alongside him. He called encouragement to Turner: "C'mon, Sergeant! Close up ranks!"

Turner managed to push Duff ahead. Rob held his end of the file back a bit, until they evened out again. Together, they surged at the attacking mob, with Stormie's reckless battle cry spurring them on.

*BOOM!*

The first explosion blew hot wind and sand at their backs. It seemed to disorient the zombies, who stopped and milled about. Jools didn't dare turn to see whether the fire had come from friend or foe. But Vanguard Frida had been watching.

"Captain! The ship's launching monster eggs!"

Now Jools did look over his shoulder. Sure enough, the big gun had been used to fire monster eggs—by the dozen. The blocks broke upon impact with the beach, hatching silverfish that immediately locked on to the human targets within range.

Rob took stock of the situation and made a snap decision. He ordered the riders to fall back and form a single file. "We'll have to give some ground to the zombies," he shouted. "We can't let the silverfish spread out into the mushrooms!"

It would be an ambush the horses couldn't overcome, Jools knew. But on an open stretch of beach, the odds would be more even. He released the reins, and Beckett responded to the captain's command to gallop on.

The horses ate up the ground between the melee site and the beach where the eggs were dropping, not far from Volt and Stormie's cannon turret. Although angry arthropods ran wild just a few blocks away, Volt valiantly provided cover when he saw the battalion coming.

*BAH-bah-bah, BAH-bah-bah, BAH-bah-bah . . . TOOM!* The repeater sent blasts of TNT in an arc around the battleship, either missing their mark in error or by Volt's design. There wasn't time to worry about his motives.

"Draw!" called Captain Rob.

The six troopers pulled the modified pitchforks Turner had crafted from their inventories. Their long handles would allow the players to skirmish from the saddle, while their mounts' armor protected them from hit damage.

"Every man for himself!" Rob cried. "Wait for it!"

There was no need to charge. The silverfish were coming for them.

*Keep it together, keep it together.* "Steady, boy," Jools said to Beckett. They had drilled this maneuver before: the horses were to wade into the stream of silverfish slowly, so the troopers could make multiple, dead-on stabs. *Every target I hit means one fewer insect spawning,* Jools reminded himself.

Letting the scuttling creatures reach them before wielding their weapons was nerve wracking. But a quick glance at Frida, arch enemy of all silverfish, told Jools to wait for his moment. Frida was still collecting XP because she'd been patient the last time. *If she can do it, so can I.*

*BOOM!*

Another shower of eggs hit the beach as the first wave of silverfish struck. For an instant, Jools took his eyes off the immediate threat to look at the breaking monster eggs. Two arthropods connected with Beckett and three with Jools. Their armor minimized the damage, but here came six more! Horse and rider shook off their attackers. Jools hiked back his prong, gulped a breath, and jabbed at them. In two strikes, nine were impaled; the other two hit Jools.

On they came. Beckett half-reared and struck at a couple of attackers beneath his feet. They gave sickening cries, and then expired. Jools found the prong to be self-reloading; skewered silverfish twinkled away to nothing, making way for the next victims.

"Look!" cried Turner, holding up a pitchfork with five expiring arthropods impaled on its tines. "Five fer a dollar."

Meanwhile, the discombobulated zombies rallied and began to cover ground again. Jools caught their movement out of the corner of his eye. *We've got to wrap this up before they get here!* Being trapped in between the two mobs would mean certain death.

Explosions rocked the beach as the battleship and Volt's cannon exchanged more volleys. Still, the troopers skirmished for their lives. Jools had never concentrated so hard on his aim with so much mayhem going on around him. But he wasn't about to create more trouble for himself by grazing a target. Most jabs met two or three of them; the rare thrust stuck five.

"Yee-haw!" he heard Rob crow. "Seven with one blow!"

*Seven?* Jools held Beckett up long enough to spy the captain. Rob rode with the reins in his teeth, waving two pitchforks, their tines writhing with dying silverfish.

"Nice shootin', Tex!" called Stormie.

The weapons Kim had designed were doing their jobs. Amid shouts of pain came tallies of the dead, similar to Robs'. In what seemed like an interminable moment, Jools felt the tide turn. Fewer arthropods remained than spawned. As the moments passed, Jools fervently hoped that Termite was out of spawn-egg bombs.

Captain Rob yelled, "I need someone to clean up these last silverfish. We must push back the zombies!"

Volt crawled out of the cannon turret. "Toss me a prong! I can do it."

Rob hesitated only an instant before throwing his weapon to Volt, who caught it and presented himself as a target to the lingering silverfish. Rob immediately ordered the battalion to split into squadrons and surround the remaining zombies. The ragged bunch had skirted the mushroom grove and was making for the eastern beach.

Stormie, Frida, and Turner headed their horses one way; Jools, Kim, and Rob the other. They experienced a second wind, dealing mighty damage to the oncoming legions. But the zombies fought back with high-grade swords that took a toll on what was left of the troopers' hearts.

"Uuuuhh, OOOHH! *Uuuuhh . . . UUUUHH!*"

As their numbers dwindled, their outraged groans increased. Jools couldn't tell whether the monsters made more noise before or after they were hit. After a time, Jools recognized the note of defeat in the ungodly din. "Press on, mates!" he yelled. "We've got them on the run!"

"Front into line!" Rob called once more. Battalion Zero again formed an impenetrable wall of armored horses and soldiers. They made a clean sweep, knocking zombies together in a writhing pool of doom, lopping off pieces of them until the whole mass was one grotesque pile of nearly dead, undead bodies.

As they quivered in their fatal throes, Frida gave a sharp warning. "Battalion! One more!"

Another jockey approached them at a mad gallop. The rider appeared to be human, but for a set of huge wings that jutted outward. The mount appeared equine . . . but was not alive.

Turner refused to believe his eyes. "What the heck—?"

"It's Lady Craven," whispered Stormie.

"On a zombie horse!" screamed Kim.

\*

Again, Jools cursed the effective night vision potion that allowed him to make out the dark-green form of four-legged decay. The grim horse and rider encountered the pit trap that had snuffed out the baby zombies, and jumped it, cleanly. As they topped a rise, Lady Craven pulled up her mount where the entire battalion could see her silhouetted against the moonlit bay.

Then the ghoulish animal rocked back and rose on its hind legs, rearing and pawing at the sky until a chunk of hoof broke off. Heedless of the damage, Lady Craven loosed the reins and set the beast running full tilt at the battalion.

Kim saw red. Griefers had kindled her intense hatred of any player who would enslave a horse in a state somewhere between life and death.

"She's *mine!*" yelled the diminutive horse master, spurring Nightwind forward.

"Oh, no she's not," Jools growled, kicking Beckett into a dead run behind her.

*Boom! . . . Boom! . . . BOOM!*

The series of blasts seemed to light the horses' hooves on fire. They raced over the mycelium flats at Lady Craven and her surreal steed. The tip of Kim's sword was a mere three blocks from the griefer queen when her wings fanned out, locking into place like a guardian's spikes. Then the charging horse and rider sailed over the two troopers' heads toward the water's edge.

The rest of the battalion had retreated to take cover from the boat's attack. Kim and Jools let Nightwind and Beckett slow as they watched Lady Craven's horse plunge into the surf and swim for the battleship.

"But Overworld horses don't swim!" Kim said to Jools, incredulous.

"That griefer's cheats have cheats," he said curtly, watching until he could no longer distinguish the pair from the dark water. The troopers turned their horses back toward their mates.

*Bah-bah-BOOM!*

A final detonation filled the air. Everyone braced—for more silverfish, for pulverized earth, for bodily damage . . . for death.

Instead, they saw the battleship lurch. One of its guns snapped off and clattered to the deck in a resounding *clang*. A fire broke out and began to spread as the ship's hull dropped in the water. Gradually, the whole thing listed off to one side.

Cheers swept over the sands. Stormie and Frida embraced. Rob and Turner high-fived, and then thumped each other on the backs. Volt wandered over to them and stood with his hands in his pockets, looking out to sea, watching the damage he'd wrought to the griefer warship. A small boat could be seen racing away from it, out to sea.

"Whoa. That was a close one," Jools said. He slid weakly from Beckett's saddle, dropped his reins, and offered Kim a hand down from Nightwind.

"Some of your best work, Lieutenant," Kim praised him modestly.

"Some of *our* best work," he corrected, gesturing at their friends.

"There's just one thing I'd like to know," Kim murmured.

"What's that?"

"What was it you said to Volt? To get him to play for our side?"

"Old Whit?" Jools loosened Beckett's girth a notch and grinned. "I forgave him."

Kim didn't reply, but he could see she was impressed.

"Not in so many words," Jools added.

Kim cocked her head.

"I asked him if he'd like to go bowling sometime. Said I'd let him keep score." *Sometimes,* Jools thought, *you just have to trust a fellow.*

Kim shrugged.

"Don't worry," said Jools. "He knew what I meant."

# CHECK OUT THE REST OF THE DEFENDERS OF THE OVERWORLD SERIES
# AND JOIN BATTALION ZERO'S QUEST:

The Battle of Zombie Hill

NANCY OSA

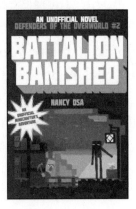

Battalion Banished

NANCY OSA

Spawn Point Zero

NANCY OSA